Praise for *One Hundred Shadows*

"There is an unforgettable, curious beauty to be found here."
—Han Kang, Winner of the Man Booker International Prize

"The South Korean's first novel—and her first to be translated into English—is mesmerizing and surreal."—*Vulture*

"Affecting [. . .] It's rare for a story to be so dense in social meaning yet so lightly composed."—*The Nation*

"Haunting [. . .] subtle but potent [. . .] a delicately-structured critique of capitalism."
—*3:AM Magazine*

"Hwang Jungeun's *One Hundred Shadows* is too odd to be this tender, and too sharply materialist to be this mystical, and too lyrical to be this gritty [. . .] The novel's symbols are as compelling as they are opaque, and it sucked me up and spat me out a different person."

—Aaron Bady, *Literary Hub*

Praise for *I'll Go On*

"Enthralling and poetic, with sentences that thrum full of melancholy and an understated intelligence that isn't afraid to ask the vital questions of who and why we are."
—Sharlene Teo

"A profound, lyrical incantation [. . .] What could be a fairly depressing story is raised to a thing of crystalline incandescence because of the sensitivity and humanity with which both author and translator craft this work."—*Translating Women*

"*I'll Go On* tenderly and poetically examines the bonds of sisterhood and family— the one we're born with and the one we choose—exploring both the damage love can do and its capacity for healing. It's at once sad and hopeful, quiet and yet full to the brim of an intense and beautiful energy."—Sophie Mackintosh

T0021454

also in english by hwang jungeun

Kong's Garden

One Hundred Shadows

I'll Go On

DD's Umbrella

years and years

年年歲歲

by Hwang Jungeun

Translated by Janet Hong

Curated by Janet Hong for the 2024 Translator Triptych

OPEN LETTER

LITERARY TRANSLATIONS FROM THE UNIVERSITY OF ROCHESTER

Library of Congress Catalog-in-Publication Data: Available.

ISBN (pb): 978-1-960385-00-0 | ISBN (ebook): 978-1-960385-05-5

The translation of this book is supported in part by the Literature Translation Institute of Korea.

 LITERATURE TRANSLATION INSTITUTE OF KOREA

This project is also supported in part by an award from the New York State Council on the Arts with the support of the governor of New York and the New York State Legislature

NEW YORK STATE OF OPPORTUNITY. | **Council on the Arts**

Printed on acid-free paper in Canada

Cover design by Eric Wilder

Open Letter is the University of Rochester's nonprofit, literary translation press.

www.openletterbooks.org

contents

gravedig 9

words to say 31

nameless 54

things to come 91

.

afterword 115

years and years

年年歳歳

gravedig

After the Chuseok holiday, before the ground freezes.

So Yi Sunil had said numerous times, and now the time had come. It was the second week of November. At six o'clock in the morning, Han Sejin got in her car and sped along the mostly empty Olympic Highway and arrived at Sunil's apartment. She pulled up to the shuttered garage and turned off the engine. Her seat chilled almost immediately. The day was bitterly cold. It would get a little warmer when the sun rose fully, but they were heading toward the MDL—the Military Demarcation Line—where the temperature, even at midday, was lower than at nights in the city. It was the same every year.

Sejin peered down at the cracked, uneven surface of the parking lot and retied her hair. She went up to the fourth floor. Sunil was waiting, everything already packed. Containers of mung bean pancakes, stuffed chili peppers, and stir-fried beef were stacked inside a paper shopping bag, along with some apples and pears, and a bottle of liquor. Next to the bag sat a smaller backpack. She'd said she wanted to use plates this time. Not Styrofoam or aluminum foil trays, but real plates, since this visit was to be their last. As soon as Sejin picked up the backpack, it sagged under the weight of the dishes, and there was a clatter.

They're going to break. Don't you care?

Why would they break? They won't, as long as you're careful, Sunil said, adding, I'm bringing them back.

Sejin said no more and carried the bags down.

After loading the bags in the trunk and spreading out a blanket in the backseat, Sejin started the car and turned on the heater. When Sunil finally appeared from the entrance of the mid-rise, Sejin was crouched in front of the car, examining the ground. Two rusted screws, dull and as fat as a thumb, protruded from the asphalt. They were all that remained of the parking barrier. Sejin's brother-in-law had installed it to prevent people from parking illegally in their lot, but it must have been a hassle for both him and the tenants to get in and out, because it was removed one day, leaving behind these two screws anchored deep into the ground. They weren't too sharp, but sharp enough to puncture a tire if a car drove over them at a certain angle. On her last visit, Sejin had mentioned they could be dangerous, and Sunil had said she'd relay the message.

They're still here, Sejin said, standing up.

Sunil frowned, shaking her head.

Did that mean she'd told her son-in-law, but he'd done nothing? Or that she hadn't mentioned it yet, because she hadn't found the right moment to bring it up? Without saying anything further, Sejin helped Sunil into the backseat, taking the duralumin cane from her and stowing it in the trunk. She then removed Sunil's right shoe, helping her prop her leg onto the center console and covering her swollen knee with a blanket. Sunil was wearing a wool cap with a small brim, a pair of thick quilted pants, a cardigan with a dizzying red-and-brown pattern, and a skinny knit-scarf wrapped around her neck.

You won't get cold dressed like that?

Sunil patted her belly, saying she had many layers on underneath. She'd also packed hiking boots, which she'd found stored neatly in a box. They belonged to Sejin's older sister, Yeongjin, who had worn them only once. Although they were a little big, as long as Sunil put on an extra pair of socks before setting out, they should fit just fine. At last, they left.

They headed northeast. If they traveled 100 kilometers an hour, they would arrive at their destination in two and a half hours. Grandfather's grave was in Jigyeong-ri village, in the town of Galmal in Cheorwon County, Gangwon Province. Both women called him Grandfather, but he was actually Sunil's grandfather, which made him Sejin's great-grandfather. He was buried deep in the mountainside where a frontline military unit was now stationed. The graves of other Jigyeong-ri residents lay scattered over the mountain as well. They needed to pass through the military base in order to access the graves. And so, every year around Chuseok, villagers gathered in front of the base, carrying sickles and bundles of food. After leaving their IDs at the checkpoint, they hiked up the mountain to hold memorial ceremonies in honor of their ancestors, each family escorted by one or two armed soldiers. Since the mid-eighties, Sunil had visited her grandfather's grave every year without fail, and once Sejin got her driver's license and a car of her own, mother and daughter would drive together. Now when Chuseok drew near, Sunil would give an old neighbor from the village a call and ask when everyone was planning to head up the mountain. Then she'd call Sejin and update her on the plan for that year's visit.

Hey, let's have some gotgam.

Sunil pulled off the stem and tore the dried persimmon in two. She held it out to Sejin, who accepted it without taking her eyes off the road. The car continued to glide forward. The sun was rising and, to their right, the mountain fog was creeping down toward the rice paddies spread below. Sejin said they weren't going to be late after all, since there was no traffic on the roads, but Sunil said they should have set out earlier—she was worried the workers had already headed up the mountain.

We need to make the last offering before they start digging.

Sunil was born in Galgol, north of Jigyeong-ri, but after she lost her parents she went to live with her grandfather in Jigyeong-ri. Some of her relatives had disappeared without a trace in the border clashes that took place along the 38th parallel during the Korean War, and her grandfather, her only remaining next of kin, took in the five-year-old Sunil, raising her and getting her to run errands for him. When she was fifteen, she was sent to live with a distant relative in Gimpo, and there she helped at a market until she married Han Jungeon, in a match arranged by one of the merchants. Sunil liked to tell Sejin how she'd never in her wildest dreams expected her grandfather to make the long, inconvenient journey to see her get married, but he'd come after all, dressed in his well-worn traditional coat. He'd sat in the wedding hall for a bit, eaten some noodles, and then left.

Grandfather passed away in Jigyeong-ri in 1978. At daybreak, three or four men from the village had shouldered his coffin and buried him halfway up the mountain. Sejin had never met him, but she knew what he looked like. A framed photo of him hung on the wall of Sunil's apartment, along with their family pictures. In the portrait, he had a scruffy beard and wore a fabric skullcap over coarse, white hair. Just from his face and expression alone, one could tell he was very short, and his forehead, eyebrows, eyes, and nose were round, like Sunil's. He seemed like someone Sejin had met many times, perhaps because she'd grown up staring at his picture her entire life. So she visited his grave every year, as if she were checking in on him. But before Sejin got her license, Sunil had made the trip alone by transferring buses several times. Neither her husband, Jungeon, nor her eldest daughter, Yeongjin, had any desire to accompany her, and Mansu, her only son and the youngest of her three children, had been too little to go with her.

Why do you go through all that trouble year after year?

Yeongjin and Jungeon couldn't understand why Sunil went to such lengths to visit her grandfather's grave. How could they possibly know about the dried-up burrows or the shrubs draped occasionally with snakes, and how, in just a year, the weeds would have grown as tall as a person and they'd have to hack them down with a sickle in order to pass through? Or about the moss and the trees twisted from lack of sunlight, the burial mound crushed and trampled by wild boars, the chestnut trees surrounding the grave, or the silence of pine trees? Sejin alone knew the reason why Sunil went up the mountain every year, cutting a path through the forest. It was her home. For her mom, that grave was her childhood home.

Grandfather, I'm a granny now. I don't know if I'll be able to come next year.

For the past few years, this is what Sunil has been saying at the graveside, but this visit was truly her last. She was seventy-two years old and planned to have knee replacement surgery on both knees next year. Once a child of the mountains, she'd been surefooted on steep terrain, harvesting fiddleheads and young shoots off angelica trees, but now she needed a cane even on flat land, and she walked slowly, grimacing from the pain. She'd held out for several years, saying each time it was her last, but she couldn't manage the wild, rugged terrain anymore and had finally accepted the truth earlier this year. After worrying about Grandfather's resting place, deserted deep in the mountains, she resolved to dig up his remains and get rid of the grave altogether. After all, no one would visit him once she was gone.

.

Two men were hired to dig and collect the remains—farmers from around Jigyeong-ri, who still lived in the village where they'd been born. Sunil called them *Mister*. When Sejin asked if they ran a funeral business on the side, Sunil said, no, but that they'd always helped with those things, so they knew what to do. She whispered the whole time, as if worried someone might overhear. The reason they had waited until after Chuseok was because the men had been busy with their own holiday preparations and ancestral memorial ceremonies, aside from looking after their harvest and livestock. As mother and daughter spoke of these things, the took the expressway and continued up north.

So when are you going to move back home? Sunil asked.

Too busy changing lanes to avoid a truck loaded with uncovered construction materials, Sejin couldn't hear what Sunil said.

What did you say?

I said, how long are you planning on living alone? Don't you think it's time you moved back home and started taking over the housework?

Me?

Who'll do it when I'm gone?

Exactly. Who would?

You! Your sister's got her own housework, so you've got to do it.

Well, I've got my own to worry about too.

You call that housework?

What do you call it then?

You're not even married.

Then what would you call looking after your own place? I'm busy with my own housework, so how can I look after yours?

That's why I'm telling you to hurry up and move back home, so I can teach you before I die.

Why do you keep saying you're going to die?

I'll be lucky if I live another five or ten years.

You're being ridiculous. Don't talk that way.

You calling your mom ridiculous?

Well, you're saying ridiculous things.

Watch it.

Sunil finished the gotgam and crumpled the empty plastic bag in one hand. Heaving a sigh, she said she'd bought the gotgam to put in some persimmon punch, but she'd ended up nibbling away at them, too busy to even boil the cinnamon sticks to make punch. There was always a mountain of work to be done in Sunil's kitchen, where pots and large stainless-steel mixing bowls smeared with marinade were stacked together. In that kitchen, Sunil cooked for two families—her and Jungeon's, as well as her daughter Yeongjin's family, who lived directly above on the top floor of the five-story, piloti-type building that belonged to Yeongjin's in-laws. Three years ago, Sunil and Jungeon had moved into the building to help their daughter with housework and the kids, since the younger couple both worked full-time. Every day Sunil would wake up in the early morning hours to prepare breakfast for Jungeon, who worked as an apartment security guard. Before she could even clean up, she would climb up to the fifth floor to make breakfast again. There, she helped her five- and three-year-old grandchildren get ready for preschool, rushing back and forth between the two floors to cook and clean, too busy to remove her dirty apron. Sometimes, during the day, she would call Sejin and talk about how cooking, cleaning, and hanging laundry consumed her entire day, because she wasn't able to move as easily as before.

Your brother-in-law has no appetite. He's so picky and he eats like a bird, Sunil often said. He takes one look at the breakfast and just picks at a few things. Or he rushes out after wolfing down a bowl of instant noodles. I never thought I'd be living at my son-in-law's house at this age, constantly walking on eggshells.

She voiced her complaints only to Sejin. She couldn't say these things to Yeongjin, and Mansu was too far away. At times, Sejin felt responsible for Sunil's exhaustion, as if her own incompetence were to blame for her mother's weariness and clammy Crocs, but most of the time, she simply listened to these laments, saying, All right, Mom, all right.

They arrived just after nine. Sejin veered off the concrete road that led to the military base and drove onto the dirt lot, which would take them to the rice paddies. She parked in the shadow of a building that resembled a small pagoda, as if she were hiding the car. It was likely a shed for storing farm equipment, with a slate door that was coming off the hinges. While Sejin gazed at it, Sunil made a phone call.

They already headed up the mountain, Sunil said as she hung up, looking anxious. He's coming down to meet us.

Sejin climbed out of the car and started unloading the trunk. Sunil put on another pair of socks, then the hiking boots. They stood in the uneven grooves formed by the cultivator tires and stared at the paddy before them. The dirt was dark brown, mottled with frost in places, the mountain surging up behind it.

He's heading down right now?

That's what he said.

Does he even know where we are? I mean, look at the size of this field.

He said he's coming.

While they stared vacantly at the base of the mountain, a man with a sickle emerged from between the bushes about fifty meters from where they stood. He waved, beckoning them to make their way across the paddy. It was Kim Geunil, the neighbor Sunil had called every year about the annual visit. The two women started to cut across the paddy where only rice stumps remained. Geunil hacked at the undergrowth, and when they reached him, he said the men had already started digging.

This early? Sunil cried.

Nine o'clock isn't early around here! We went up at the crack of dawn.

He told them to follow him. After rubbing the mud from her shoes onto the dry grass, Sejin stared at the spot in the bushes where he'd just disappeared. The slope was steep. Would her mother be able to manage it? Sejin glanced about for flatter terrain but found none, and with no sign of Geunil, who seemed to have moved far ahead, Sejin set down her backpack and shopping bag, and faced Sunil. After she'd pushed her mother through the dense undergrowth, slipping several times and nearly falling herself, she picked up the bags once more and climbed up the slope. Autumn was in full swing. The ground was spongy with leaves that lay rotting where they had fallen, untouched by human feet, but at times dry branches hidden under the leaves snapped, jabbing their ankles. Saplings that had germinated from the seeds of big trees were growing in the shade, their branches sticking out at unpredictable angles. Wrapping her left fist with the small blanket she'd brought to sit on, Sejin led the way, pushing thin branches aside so that Sunil would have an easier time moving through the foliage.

Geunil came back down the steep incline to check on mother and daughter, who were lagging far behind, and then went ahead again. His navy-blue jacket and gray hair flashed between the trees. If Sejin and Sunil lost sight of him, they simply stood still and listened for the hacking of his sickle to guide them. Only once they arrived at the gravesite did their surroundings look somewhat familiar.

The burial mound was already gone and in its place was a deep, narrow pit. At the edge was a heap of fine loam, and a worker in rubber boots was digging inside the hole, which was as deep as he was tall. Sejin saw Sunil's face twist with pain, and then annoyance—none of which she dared to express.

Oh Mister, I was going to make an offering first, Sunil protested, putting on a bright voice.

Don't worry, we offered up some liquor already, said a worker crouched beside the dirt pile, watching the other worker dig. And you can do it later when we take the remains down. For the cremation.

They had come up the mountain at six in the morning and been digging for three hours. One was wearing rubber boots and the other a cap thickly embroidered with the National Agricultural Cooperative Federation logo. They were old, around the same age as Sunil, with tanned faces and sunken cheeks. Though small and thin, they were skilled with the shovel. They dug as small an area as possible to cut down on unnecessary work, but they hadn't found the remains yet. They worried whether they might be digging in the wrong spot. It was now nine fifty. Geunil said they should be hitting the pine branches first.

We put the body in and then covered it with pine branches. That's what we did back then. Only the rich folks got buried in coffins—stone coffins that don't rot. But that's all a waste, does no good, because tree roots will go through even stone.

The worker in the boots climbed out of the pit and the one in the cap hopped in. The digging continued. Sunil paced around the grave with her cane, eventually joining Sejin on the ground under the pine tree, where she'd sat after setting down the bags. Sejin helped her mother sit. They looked toward the grave and listened to Geunil talk with the workers.

The ground's full of roots.

Pine?

Yup.

At least you can cut through pine. Imagine if it was acacia.

Whew! Acacia's tough. This is soft at least.

That's right, pine roots are soft.

I came here with your father a long time ago, Sunil said. We took the bus. Back then the roads weren't paved, so we traveled for over two hours on roads so thick with dust you couldn't see out the window. There was no easy way to the grave like now, so we had to go round and round along the mountain ridge. When we finally arrived and were about to perform the bows, I found your father standing over there, facing the other way, with his hands clasped behind his back. I asked him what he was doing and told him to get over here and offer up a bow, but then he said some hogwash about how a man isn't supposed to even pull weeds at the gravesite of his wife's family. Boy, I just about lost it! I told him to show his respect to Grandfather right this minute, but he kept standing there with his hands behind his back. I'd never been so mortified and disgusted. I didn't ask him to come after that. That was the one and only time he came with me.

She pulled a small pine cone out from under her, then clenched and unclenched it, kneading it as if it were a lump of dough, and finally tossed it toward the western slope. It disappeared between the trees with a thump. She said that over there was Galgol, which Sejin already knew. She'd never been, but her mother pointed it out every year.

In Galgol, there was a mountain that Sunil had inherited. Though it had belonged to her father, who had died when she was little, it had been reported as an unregistered mountain and nearly become government property, but thanks to the testimonies of the neighborhood elders, she'd been able to prove her ownership. She'd then registered the mountain in her husband Jungeon's name and he planned to leave it to their son Mansu. Jungeon never forgot to pay the property tax and stored the title deed in a safe place, making various calls every year to see if the mountain had gone up in value. Since it was difficult for people and equipment to access, it had very little value, and even if he were to put it up for sale, no one was likely to buy it. Still, he considered that mountain a source of great pride. And he planned to leave it all to his son.

Mansu was admitted into the English literature program at a university in Gyeonggi Province. After completing his studies with the help of a scholarship, which he received sporadically, he began looking for a job, but failed to get past the interview stage each time. Sejin remembered how, after he'd come back from an interview, he'd crouched down in his suit, which hung a little baggy on his tall, lanky frame, and patted an old dog on the head. This was back when they all still lived at home, except for Yeongjin. He was living in New Zealand now, taking courses to earn a professional certificate. Once he completed his certification, he said he'd be able to find a job right away, a well-paying one. Sejin sent him a bit of allowance sometimes, while Yeongjin sent him money for tuition. But even with his sisters' help, it wasn't enough to cover everything, so he'd always had to work while attending school, though he didn't seem as discouraged as he'd been in Korea.

I think he's adjusted well, Yeongjin said often, and Sejin thought the same. In Korea, he'd been in low spirits with no breathing space, but he seemed to have found his niche now. They could tell just by his expressions and voice during their video calls. Mansu regularly updated his sisters, telling them how he was gaining experience by working part-time in a prospective field. He came home once every one and a half to two years, bearing gifts like Cadbury chocolates, Comvita Manuka honey lozenges, or Manuka honey. He would stay for about three weeks, either at Yeongjin's place or downstairs with his parents, before leaving again.

Sejin didn't think he would move back to Korea just to inherit the mountain. What would he do with land where you weren't allowed to gather so much as a single acorn? In fact, what would anyone do with a mountain like—

Vapor rose from the pit. The sun was shining directly onto the grave, and it steamed in the light, as if someone had poured hot water inside.

I heard a grave isn't supposed to steam like that during a dig, Sunil said worriedly.

Geunil, who'd been watching from the edge of the pit with crossed arms, said it was actually pretty common. Because it's warmer underground and this is a sunny spot.

Sunil propped herself up with her cane and walked toward him.

Still nothing?

Nope, not yet. We should have hit some dark soil by now.

They must have buried him real deep.

Yeah, guess so.

Poor Grandfather. He had a hard life.

Everyone had a hard life back then. Things are still hard, but at least we're not going hungry. There used to be times when there just wasn't enough to eat.

Sejin watched the worker fling several shovelfuls of dirt out of the pit, but when the color of the soil changed, she got up from under the pine tree. The dirt was no longer fine, brittle, reddish clay, but clumps of yellow and black soil. Fragments of what looked like dark wood were mixed in. Geunil and the second digger started to comb through the dirt for bones. Sunil hovered around them, and after they had finished, she picked through the dirt again to make sure they hadn't left any pieces behind.

Make sure you get all the dark soil, Geunil said. All of it.

They spread a square of white rayon over the leaves and pine cones covering the ground and laid the bones on top. Two shinbones, more or less intact, fragments of a skull resembling chunks of coconut shell, and small lumps that looked like pebbles. There weren't many pieces. Before they filled the pit, Sunil tossed a coin inside. The diggers started sweeping the dirt that was piled on the edge back into the hole. Side by side, Sejin and Sunil watched as the men wasted no time in filling the hole. They planted a sapling on the flat surface, which was neither a burial mound nor a pit anymore. Sejin thought it looked like a pine sapling. Stuck in a sunny, exposed spot, it seemed likely to topple over very soon.

•

A year after Mansu had moved to New Zealand, he shared that he had become quite close to an elderly Caucasian gentleman. A tremendous bibliophile, he sometimes cooked elaborate meals for Mansu, and they even went camping together on weekends. Mansu sent photos taken in the old man's house in Auckland. Even the hallway was lined with shelves full of books. Dressed in corduroy pants and an argyle sweater, a plump man with a short beard smiled beside Mansu. On his last visit, Mansu brought a present from this man for Sunil. It was around Christmas time, and they had gathered in Yeongjin's apartment to celebrate his homecoming and the holiday season.

When Sejin finally arrived and stepped into the living room, she saw Sunil seated on the sofa, surrounded by family. On her lap, knees pressed together as if worried about dropping it, was a large ceramic platter. She held it carefully, a shy smile on her lips. The clay seemed to have been roughly kneaded, and the old man had painted vines and bunches of grapes on its surface, which had then been glazed.

Come look at this, Sunil said to Sejin, grasping the platter with both hands. That book collector told Mansu to give it to me.

Sejin picked up the platter and peered at the artwork, turning it over to glance at the bottom. The platter was extremely thick and heavy. Yeongjin stretched out her hands, saying she wanted to have another look. Sejin handed it over and opened the old man's second gift, an herbal candy tin. A piece of black sponge covered the bottom of the can and on it lay a faded gold pendant. Telling them it had belonged to an old woman who'd been a Holocaust survivor, Mansu relayed the old man's message: "You, Mother, are great. You are great."

While the family examined the gifts, curious about their sender, Sunil got up from the sofa as if embarrassed and went into the kitchen. Sejin saw Sunil swipe her thumbs over her cheeks as she put on an apron. Steam rose from a pot on the stove, and a basket lined with parchment paper was filled with both beef and vegetable patties, and there were japchae noodles that even included thin strips of egg. It truly was a feast. They joined two tables normally reserved for memorial services to make one long table in the living room, set it with food, and ate to their heart's content.

Ah, I missed this, Mansu said with a bright smile. You don't know how much I missed it.

You are great.

When Sejin first heard those words, she was bewildered, but she soon felt a surge of anger, as if horns were sprouting from her forehead. Later she pondered what it was that she'd felt, why she'd felt that way, and why those words had seemed like an insult. Perhaps it was her brother's choice of Korean. He would have heard those words in English, and maybe that was part of the reason, but to her, his words sounded patronizing, like a king with a sceptre making a declaration.

That night, as Sunil went back and forth between the kitchen and living room, she seemed busier and more animated than usual. Sejin noticed that her mother, though preoccupied, blushed at times, lost in thought, perhaps thinking about the message that Mansu had relayed, looking as if she might burst into tears at any moment. After dinner, Mansu mentioned he'd been interviewed by Auckland's local news station for being a model immigrant and played the clip he'd saved on his phone. On the screen, where the news station's logo appeared in the corner, Mansu gave an amiable smile.

Here, I was able to find possibilities and opportunities I couldn't find in my own country.

Possibilities. Opportunities. He used these words repeatedly in the interview.

Yes, of course, Sejin thought, as she rolled up her sleeves to tackle the pile of dirty dishes on the kitchen island. If he decided never to move back to Korea, she wouldn't blame him.

That evening, Mansu mentioned that the bibliophile, as well as his co-workers, were very interested in the recent political and social situation in Korea. He asked Sejin if she was planning to attend the candlelight protest taking place in downtown Seoul on Saturday. She said no, but offered to accompany him if he wished to go. That Saturday had been December 17, 2016.*

On Saturday after work, Sejin headed to Gwanghwamun. She met her brother at the Kyobo Bookstore and together they went up to the square. Mansu was impressed by the massive crowd and held his phone constantly above his head to snap pictures. He handed Sejin his phone, asking her to take some of him, making sure she captured the surroundings. She took several of Mansu in front of the people-packed steps of the Sejong Center for the Performing Arts. He scrolled through his photos, picking the one where he held the tealight cup under his chin like a microphone, and sent it to his friends in Auckland.

They left before the protest ended and headed to a restaurant. They had a pasta with roasted garlic chips and a creamy pasta with crabmeat. When she asked him somewhat awkwardly if he didn't eat food like this all the time, he said not at all, that he'd sometimes stand in the kitchen of the restaurant where he worked and wolf down leftovers, or that he'd eat plain bread at his lodgings in order to save money, but thanks to her, he was able to enjoy a proper meal at a fancy restaurant. They flipped through the wine list to choose a bottle, but put the list aside in the end.

---

* A series of candlelight protests were held in Seoul's Gwanghwamun Square from October 2016 to March 2017, demanding President Park Geun-hye's resignation. Over two million people participated in the "Candlelight Revolution," successfully pressuring the National Assembly into processing the impeachment of Park. In April 2018, Park was found guilty on multiple counts of bribery, coercion, abuse of power, and leaking classified information, and sentenced to twenty-four years in prison.

You know, New Zealand is a great place for women and older folks. Come visit with Mom and stay a while.

All right.

People are really interested in what's going on in Korea these days. Especially the candlelight protests.

She scooped up some of the browned garlic chips with her fork and mentioned the older folks who'd gathered in a corner of the square. She said one of them will no doubt get upset and take an LPG gas can into the streets. She simply couldn't understand what went on inside their heads, she really wished they would stop doing those things. Mansu said they had the right to do what they wanted.

They can express their political views, too, you know. You have no right to say they shouldn't do something, he said, swallowing a forkful of noodles. Plus, you're a little biased.

What?

Well, you lean quite a bit to one side.

Taken aback, she gazed at Mansu, finally asking him why he thought that. He glanced at her, as if surprised by her question.

Hmm, he said, thinking. Well, you're always listening to podcasts.

•

Sejin and Sunil fell behind. Because of the pain in her legs, going down the mountain proved to be more precarious for Sunil than climbing up. Taking half a step at a time, she worried they would trail too far behind the men, who had gone ahead to prepare for the cremation. She regretted letting them carry down the remains.

We should have brought them down ourselves. What if they start without me, before we get there?

In her rush, Sunil nearly fell twice. They avoided the fallen trees, the tangles of branches, spots that were much too steep, putting them farther away from their destination. Sejin led the way, laden down with the backpack. More used to seeing the city's asphalt surfaces and man-made slopes, she found it difficult to orient herself on the mountain. In the end, they found themselves in a brush of grasses and branches so entangled it was impossible to take another step.

What are you doing? Sunil said, clucking her tongue as she took the lead. She grabbed hold of the branches in her way and let go, which launched them at Sejin each time, almost whipping her in the forehead or eye.

Near the foot of the mountain, they came across a colony of acacias. The trees were still young. Each one was as straight as a pencil, and the unusually thick thorns sprouting from the thin branches were the color of steel. Sunil shuddered at the sight, but Sejin stared at them, stunned by their beauty. It looked like a graphite sketch by a skilled artist, and in some ways like a complex pattern meant to depict a different di-mension. Behind the colony of acacias was the paddy they had crossed before starting up the mountain, but the thorns prevented them from cutting through past the acacias. As they went around the colony, they found a slope Sunil could navigate and headed down that way.

When they were nearly finished crossing the paddy, Sejin heard loud crackling and smelled fire. The men were burning the bones on a bra-zier. As soon as Sejin and Sunil drew close, the men said they were almost done. Most of the pieces had been wood chips anyway, and since there weren't too many bones, they expected to finish sooner than anticipated. Pale gray ash floated around the brazier. Sunil said nothing. No longer forcing a smile to avoid offending the workers, she paced around the fire with her mouth clamped shut. The brazier was an old, blackened, rusted drum about half a meter high, and it was set crookedly on the bare ground where only rice stumps remained. A soot-covered grate was placed over the brazier, and on it were several fragments coated with ash, burning blue-hot. Geunil, standing near the brazier with a pair of extra-long tongs, inserted them into the flames to pick up one of the pieces. After examining it to see it was indeed bone and that it was sufficiently incinerated to be ground into powder, he placed it in a stone mortar beside the brazier. The second and third fragments also went into the mortar.

They did this in an inconspicuous spot where the reeds grew high. Sejin knew even the soldiers at the base checkpoint wouldn't be able to see what was happening. The vast, shorn field awaiting winter was empty, without a soul in sight. Still, there were people who lived nearby. But they'd have no idea what was brought down from the mountain, she thought.

The crackling noise faded, and the fire was extinguished. While the workers put the brazier away, Geunil took the mortar and pestle into the reeds. Sejin and Sunil hurriedly spread out a mat on the paddy field and took the plates from their backpack. They transferred the food onto the plates, as the pounding of the pestle came from the direction of the reeds. They placed the apples and pears, the dried pollack, the now-cold stir-fried beef and vegetable pancakes on separate dishes, and poured clear liquor into a small glass cup. When they finished laying out the ritual food on a plastic mat—a blue and yellow Tayo the Little Bus play mat—Sunil set her cane down and bowed, supported by Sejin. Sunil then told her to offer a bow to Grandfather, to say goodbye and ask for his blessing so that that all would go well for them. However, Sejin asked for nothing, and as she bowed, she thought that they were no longer bowing in the direction of his remains. When she raised her head after finishing her final half-bow, she saw Geunil emerging from the reeds, holding the mortar upside down and shaking out the remaining dust.

They paid the workers and said goodbye. Sunil shook Geunil's hand and sniffled, saying they probably wouldn't be seeing each other again. On their way back to the car, the sole of Sunil's hiking boot got stuck in the mud and was pulled off completely. Then, after a few more steps, the other sole also got stuck and came off. Baffled, Sejin and Sunil examined the boots, which Yeongjin had worn only once and which looked brand new. They realized the rubber on the bottom of the boots, as well as the bond, had turned gummy. The soles, stuck deep in the mud, were too difficult to retrieve, so they simply left them behind and hurried away.

On Friday evening, Mansu video-called Sejin and asked about her recent visit to Cheorwon. It was midnight where he was. He had a fleece blanket wrapped around his shoulders. He'd been having a hard time, his new apartment was infested with bedbugs and he had come down with a cold. He had recently applied for permanent residency and was optimistic about it. Once he received his green card, he planned to find a proper living space and suggested that she come visit with Sunil and Yeongjin then and stay for a long time.

All right, all right, Sejin said. She then told him about the boot soles they'd left behind in the field.

You just left them there? he cried. On someone else's property, stuck in the mud like that?

He laughed for a long time, saying it was just like Mom. Then finally he said, Thanks, Sis. Really. But you know you don't have to do everything she says, right?

What are you talking about?

Don't try so hard. No one expects you to be the perfect daughter.

Perfect?

Sejin said it wasn't that.

No, it wasn't that at all. She didn't tell her brother it would have broken anyone's heart to see their mom's face as she urged Sejin to say goodbye to Grandfather, to say goodbye for the last time. Sejin didn't say it had always been only that.

words to say

Han Yeongjin was a skilled salesperson. She could sell anything. Over-stocked canned beverages, fabric goods, ceramic plates and bowls. For the past few years, it's been bedding—comforters and pillows. Of the dozen bedding stores on the department store's ninth floor, the one that Yeongjin managed had the highest sales. She was better at selling expensive products than cheap ones. For example, moms often came looking for her specifically, and she'd show them a variety of comforters and bedding that would improve the quality of sleep, concentration, and energy level of their highschoolers who were preparing for their college entrance exams. She'd patiently explain the material and color palette to them, and the moment they seemed to come to a decision, she led them to the top-tier, luxury bedding section. After encouraging them to feel the comforters for themselves, she stood back while they ran their hands over the fabric and flipped corners. Then as they rubbed the layers between their fingers to examine the filling, she'd say in a soft voice.

It's nice, isn't it?

It is.

How about getting one for yourself?

Oh, no, I don't need it.

But it's so nice.

It sure is.

Then why not? Why should only kids get nice bedding? If anyone should have this, it's moms.

While other stores would sell a bedding set by preying on the devotion of mothers who put their families first, Yeongjin would get the moms to buy a second comforter and pillow for themselves. Envious, employees from the other stores would study Yeongjin's sales tactic and copy her, but the results were never the same. Moms should have nice bedding, too. Though they said the same thing, Yeongjin would make a sale, but not them. Even she didn't know what she did differently, but when asked what her secret was, she'd say she was a daughter who understood her mother well. I'm the eldest, you see. We didn't have much growing up, and as the pillar of my family, I always had a special bond with my mom.

•

On Friday night, Yeongjin sat across from Yi Sunil, at a table with a heavy granite top. Milky white with black streaks, the stone slab was more than five centimeters thick. It had belonged to Yeongjin's in-laws. Though it was bulky and formal, it seemed a waste to throw away a perfectly good table, so they'd had it moved to her place.

That's right, it had taken three movers to carry it up, Yeongjin thought, gazing at the rounded edges of the stone. Two of them had looked as if they were in their sixties, and the third seemed to be in his early forties at most. They'd struggled to carry the heavy table up to the fifth floor of her building, which had no elevator. It was only after she'd paid them and sent them on their way that she and Sunil discovered the scratched corner. The scratches were long and thin, like the marks left on skin scraped against pavement. When Yeongjin rubbed at them, powder came off on her fingers. Sunil was upset, though the table was neither new nor hers.

Yeongjin sat at the table now, trying to remember which corner it had been. It was past midnight. The small kitchen lamp was on, and all the bedroom lights were off. The tabletop where her elbow rested smelled of salt and water. Yeongjin hadn't taken off the stockings she'd worn all day and Sunil was still in her apron. Yeongjin knew the apron was the first thing Sunil put on after getting out of bed and the last thing she took off before going to sleep. At her daughter's home, Sunil washed dishes, tidied up the children's toys, did the laundry, mopped the floor, hung clothes to dry, and took charge of the cooking. Sunil looked after six people in total—her daughter Yeongjin, son-in-law Wonsang, their children Yeobeom and Yeobin, Sunil's husband Jungeon, and herself. She managed all the housework for two households single-handedly, making enough side dishes and soup for everyone. In exchange, Yeongjin allowed her elderly parents to live in one of the apartments downstairs and helped with their living expenses. Yeongjin also took care of her mom's affairs and put up with her grumbling.

Yeongjin gazed at the stains on Sunil's apron. They were probably oil splatters from frying the croakers. Mom, Mom, she interrupted. Go to bed. It's late.

The next morning on her way to work, Yeongjin thought about the last words from the night before. Had her mom detected something in what she'd said? A certain feeling or thought? The subway train was rattling over the Han River. A light rain was falling, and the water level seemed higher from the day before. Yeongjin liked this part of her commute. Here, she could see the gray sky on gray days, and the clear sky on clear days. She couldn't see outside at all from the department store, and she felt this affected her health. She stood holding onto a handle and gazed out, wondering if she would be able to go on a trip somewhere this coming holiday. By herself. Anywhere. A woman sitting in the seat in front of Yeongjin bent over to retrieve something from the shopping bag between her feet. Yeongjin stepped back to give her room and ended up making eye contact with the man standing next to her. He was a foreigner with dark brown hair, thick eyebrows, and brown eyes. Their eyes met again.

The color of your coat looks good on you, he said to her in Korean. There's something very special about you. You're pretty. Can I take you out on a date? I'd love to talk to you.

She ignored him, suspecting he was part of a religious group or an MLM company. Perhaps he had a fetish for Asian women, yellow coats, or bobbed hair. Very special. Pretty. It was a trick, a **dirty lie**. The woman sitting in front of Yeongjin clutched her phone and texted someone, eyeing Yeongjin and the man. Yeongjin frowned and said no in English.

No?

Yes, no.

Why?

I have a husband, I have two children, I'm in my forties. However, she didn't say any of this aloud and simply fixed her eyes straight ahead, and then got off at her stop. She walked quickly to the turnstiles. She thought something offensive and ridiculous had happened to her, but as she mulled it over amid the crowd, it didn't strike her as so offensive and ridiculous after all. It was somewhat funny, actually. Before stepping into the locker room at work, she texted her husband.

So a foreigner hit on me on the subway. He asked me out on a date.

Wonsang replied right away.

Hahaha

Maybe you heard wrong

He was probably asking "Where is the toilet?"

After reading the texts several times, she realized it wasn't the foreigner or what he'd said that she couldn't trust. Who knows? He may have lied to hide bad motives. His motives weren't important. It's me, she thought. What I couldn't trust, to the point that I got offended, wasn't him or his words, but me . . . **He couldn't possibly find me that attractive.** Her husband seemed to think so, and she thought the same. **Dirty lie.** Thinking intently about these words, she walked to her store. Bundles of blankets and parcels that had arrived early in the morning were piled carelessly in front of the store, as if they'd been tossed there. With both arms, she picked up the bundle at the top and went inside, wondering if she'd be able to sell the most expensive comforter set that day. The vacuum-sealed cotton weighed down on her chest. It was close to opening time.

One of you is telling a dirty lie.

Yeongjin remembered those words. She remembered the meaning, the tone, and the expression of the man who'd said them—her father. It had been over her money. When she was nineteen, she'd left two 10,000-won bills on her desk, but they'd gone missing. She suspected her siblings. She called Sejin and Mansu over and told them she'd left 20,000 won on the desk and asked which of them had taken the money. They both denied it, looking bewildered. You left money here? I didn't take it. Me neither. Think hard. Maybe you left it somewhere else and forgot?

Yeongjin was sure she was right. She'd left the money there only an hour earlier. She even remembered setting the bills down, thinking, What if someone takes them? However, her siblings remained gracious while being accused, which made her suspect them even more. They were guilty, she was sure of it. One of them had taken it, or they were in it together. While Yeongjin grilled them, their father came home. All three took turns explaining their side of the story to Jungeon. Yeongjin was more enraged by her siblings playing dumb than the fact that her money was missing. Just wait, Dad's going to get to the bottom of this. When he finds out who took it, he'll teach you a lesson and you'll be in big trouble. Thinking these things, she glared at her siblings. Then Jungeon spoke. One of you is telling a dirty lie.

One of you.

This is what Jungeon said, but he was looking at Yeongjin as he spoke. He had been drinking and gave off a scorched smell, and his eyes were bloodshot. With those bloodshot eyes, he glared at Yeongjin, and she couldn't forget it. She remembered it all—the fear and helplessness she felt at that moment, the shame that should not have been hers. When her own children wailed, blaming something or someone else, when they came to her to tattle on each other, desperately explaining their side of the story, Yeongjin stared at their faces and thought about those words: Dirty lie. To prevent them from flying out of her mouth, she widened her eyes and considered those words, that tone.

Her father probably didn't recall the incident. She'd been wrong to hope he would deliver a verdict. Around that time, Jungeon had been backed into a corner. He'd been on the verge of losing everything: their dried fish store in the heart of a bustling market, their products, their home. He and some other merchants at the market had been part of a private fund group, but the treasurer committed fraud and fled. Both he and Sunil were equally responsible, but Jungeon, listed as the sole owner, could not cope. Every night, he drank past his limit and returned home, hurling their possessions into the yard until he passed out from exhaustion. Their shop closed soon after.

At the time, Yeongjin, who'd been attending a liberal arts high school, was looking for a way to study fine art, but she kissed her dreams goodbye and found a job at a distributor immediately after graduating high school. She had a gift. She was a good salesperson, and by selling, she supported the family. After the turmoil passed, Jungeon brought in some income by taking on manual labor jobs here and there, but it was sporadic at best, and Yeongjin made a lot more. It was Yeongjin whom Sunil consulted whenever they needed money, whenever they needed to give cash gifts or cover a large, unexpected expense, whenever they ran into a problem. Even her siblings consulted her. Yeongjin assumed responsibility for all family matters. And since no one else could, she paid for Jungeon's gallstone surgery and Sunil's dental expenses, she took out a loan to cover the deposit for their new house, contributed to Sejin and Mansu's college tuitions, and helped with Mansu's preparations to study abroad. When Mansu had first said he wanted to go to New Zealand, she could hardly believe his nerve, but in time, she accepted it had been the better choice, instead of remaining in Korea. He said he could work the same job in New Zealand but earn three times as much. If he could meet the necessary qualifications and get work, he would repay her soon enough. Though the course requirements kept increasing, Yeongjin believed Mansu's tuition was a kind of investment. Soon enough, he would graduate and find work. She didn't know exactly what kind of work, but according to him, it would be soon.

Do you have any brighter colors?

Yeongjin was walking toward the shelf to grab some throw pillows in mint green and lemon for a customer when she spotted Sejin. She stood watching Yeongjin beside the 25% off sales rack of lightweight comforters. She had something resembling a gunnysack slung over her shoulder instead of a purse and was wearing a duffle coat that hardly looked warm enough. When their eyes met, Sejin smiled with her mouth closed, making it hard for Yeongjin to tell if she was smiling or frowning. The customer examined the pillows and then left. As Yeongjin saw the customer out, she sighed to herself. With those manners, how did her sister get along with people?

Why didn't you say hi when you came in?

I just got here.

Sejin said she'd been in the area. It was past lunchtime, but neither of them had eaten. Yeongjin took Sejin down to the employees' cafeteria. There were several nicer restaurants near the department store, but Yeongjin didn't suggest going there, and Sejin didn't insist on going out. This was Yeongjin's rule: anyone who came to visit the breadwinner at her job should see where she worked and what she did, what she ate and drank, how she earned her money. Because this was how they had been supported until now, how they were able to survive. No one had explicitly taught her this, but she'd learned from her parents at the market, from her colleagues at work.

With her wallet in hand, Yeongjin weaved between the tables. She exchanged jokes with the employees who, like her, had found time to eat only now, and led her younger sister before the menu board for the day. Bibimbap or rice noodle soup. Sejin wanted a rice noodle soup and Yeongjin opened her wallet to pay for two. She sat down and watched Sejin set her tray on the table, hang her bag on the backrest, pull out her chair, and perch delicately on the seat. Sejin's bag was dirty, to the extent that Yeongjin didn't think it required such careful handling. Judging by the footprint on the bottom corner—someone must have stepped on it—Sejin was probably in the habit of setting it down on the ground without much thought. You could do that with a comfortable bag—set it down anywhere at any time, though who knew how comfortable it actually was? She watched her sister, thinking, Why on earth would she carry that thing around? Sejin stuck her arm in the bag and pulled out two books. She held them out, saying they were for Yeongjin's children. Yeongjin flipped through them and saw they were picture books without any text. When she asked why Sejin had bought two copies of the same book, Sejin looked bewildered. Because you have two kids. Yeongjin flipped through the pages and closed the book.

How about you give them to the kids yourself?

When? It's hard for me to get there.

It's too far out of the way, she added, but Yeongjin sensed Sejin wanted to avoid her brother-in-law. Recently, Wonsang hadn't been greeting Yeongjin's side of the family properly. He'd sit buried in the living room sofa and say hi with the briefest eye contact, or he wouldn't bother coming out of his room under the excuse that he was sleeping. She left him alone since he wasn't the type to do something just because she asked him to. Yeongjin looked down at her bowl and ate her noodles. There wasn't enough room on the table for their two trays, so she had to place her left elbow on the picture books. Sejin said she planned to go to New Zealand next year to see glaciers and penguins. And I'll check on Mansu too. She asked if Yeongjin wanted to come along, but Yeongjin said no.

I don't have time and I don't even have a passport. She remained silent for some time, but feeling bad for her blunt response, she finally said, Glaciers and penguins? Why would you go all the way there to see them?

Because that's where they are.

You want to see them that bad?

Yup.

Why?

You don't?

But why do you want to see them?

Why, Yeongjin wondered, as she gazed into her bowl. Why would Sejin spend that kind of money to go there? Especially to see those things? With her chopsticks, Yeongjin picked up the bean sprouts at the bottom of her bowl and then let them drop. How about Mom, she asked. How about you take Mom along? I think she'd like that. Sejin said nothing for a moment, then said she'd think about it.

She saw Sejin off, who gave a small wave before turning to leave. With the picture books tucked under her arm, Yeongjin walked through the aisles to head back to her store. The sharp corners of the books stabbed her in the side. She regretted having said the last bit to Sejin. I shouldn't have brought up Mom. But this sort of thing usually happened when she talked to Sejin. She would become awkward, then upset over what she shouldn't have said and what she hadn't planned to say, but ended up saying anyway.

Sejin was different from Yeongjin in many ways. Unlike Yeongjin, who from a young age went around as the ringleader with her large groups of friends, Sejin was mostly alone. But this didn't make her sad, and she didn't seem to think it was a problem. Yeongjin liked cold noodles, while Sejin preferred hot. Sejin could drink piping hot tea, but

Yeongjin couldn't bring anything hot to her lips. Yeongjin gravitated toward bright colors, whereas Sejin inclined toward neutral ones. Sejin was taller than Yeongjin, and even their physiques were different. They had many other differences, but they wore the same shoe size. When they were in high school and lived under the same roof, they would wear each other's running shoes. No, Yeongjin would usually wear her sister's, but Sejin said nothing. She'd simply wear whichever pair was left. She wouldn't even get angry at Yeongjin, or tell her not to touch her things. But it had probably bothered Sejin. At least a little. Recently Yeongjin found herself thinking about this, and her face would turn red. She felt as though she'd wronged her little sister. As though she'd left her sister behind in the distant past. Even if she were to apologize to the adult Sejin now, Yeongjin didn't think she could reach that child from back then.

Sejin moved out at the start of her second semester during her freshman year of college. According to her, three or four of her friends in a "similar" situation had pooled their money to lease a "workspace." Sejin lived there until she was able to move out and get a rental unit of her own. After graduating from college, she wrote plays while working various jobs. A few of her plays had been produced so far, and Yeongjin had gone to see one of them.

It had been her first time watching a play in a theater. Thinking she'd better wear formal clothing, she dressed with care, left work a little earlier than usual, and headed to the theater. The small theater was located deep underground and didn't hold many people. Yeongjin sat nervously in the seat Sejin had reserved for her, waiting for the performance to start. The play was about a family that had gathered for dinner. There was a low, wide table in the middle of the stage, with the actors sitting around it on the floor, eating, drinking, and talking. The scene depicted an ordinary family dinner, with no significant action. From time to time, roars could be heard in the background, as if several sounds had been combined and stretched out. The performers acted as if they couldn't hear the noise, even when it was so loud that their own lines couldn't be heard. The noise itself seemed to have an important role in the play. Yeongjin refrained from covering her ears with her hands and watched the stage. Gradually, she realized she recognized the scene.

Yes, Yeongjin knew this scene.

There she was on stage, along with Wonsang, Sunil, Sejin, Mansu, and Jungeon. Multiple evenings and situations seemed to have been blended together, but it was roughly their Christmas dinner from a year ago. Around that time, the department store had been so busy they needed extra workers.

Just come work for me, Yeongjin said to Sejin. If you work hard, I can pay you up to two and a half million won a month.

Don't be ridiculous, Wonsang said from across the table, raising his face toward the stage lights. How're you going to give her that much? You think you've got that kind of power?

The actor who was playing Yeongjin squeezed her eyes shut, as if trying to suppress her emotions, and then opened them again. Yeongjin tried to remember if she'd done the same back then, made that kind of expression.

Someone sharp, who catches on quick, cried Yeongjin from the stage, peering intently at Sejin's face. The actor hollered, as if trying to make herself heard over the deafening background roar. That's what I need right now. Someone who gets me.

Yeongjin stifled a giggle, listening to the actor repeat what had been her words. It made her feel strange, embarrassed, and shy. And emotional as well. There was nothing funny about the scenario, but she felt as though she might burst into laughter at any second. Wonsang said he had to go to the bathroom. She watched as he stuck his behind out in a slapstick fashion and plop himself down on Yeongjin's back, sitting on her, as he made his way down from the stage. Someone sitting near her muttered, Fucking asshole.

Yeongjin turned around in her seat and saw people's faces. The faces of strangers, who were witnessing her, a stranger, at this very moment. The stage lighting suddenly turned pink, and the faces glowed pink. Flinching in shock, she turned away from their faces to once again watch the stage, where the actor playing Yeongjin still remained.

When the play ended and the audience rose to their feet, Yeongjin followed. She was swept along with the crowd toward the narrow aisle, but right before she exited the theater, she stepped off to the side. She looked toward the front of the theater. The actors and staff had come out from backstage and were greeting their guests. Sejin was also on stage. Under the lighting, her faint eyebrows appeared even fainter. With her hair tied in a low ponytail, she seemed to be calmly describing something, surrounded by three or four people from the audience. They looked like friendly people. Yeongjin assumed they were the friends Sejin had shared the workspace with in college. Sejin's arms were full of roses wrapped in cellophane and colored paper that they'd handed her. Realizing she had come empty-handed to her sister's performance, Yeongjin felt embarrassed. She lingered a little while longer, then finally slipped out of the theater. She walked, feeling the cool night breeze, and stepped into the first coffeeshop she saw. She sat next to the window and leaned back against the sofa. Outside, several young people walked by, chattering with one another. Yeongjin wondered if they had also seen the play, if they had been sitting near her. She was so tired she couldn't move.

A little while later, she pulled out the playbill from her purse and peered at it again. *Family Exercise*. That was the name of the play.

He's not a bad person, she thought, slipping her arms inside the folded comforter to spread it open. Wonsang wasn't that bad. He grumbled about Sunil having too many potted plants on the rooftop, about the weight of those pots filling with water when it rained, potentially causing the roof to cave in or leak, and he grimaced at Jungeon's growing pile of junk in the garage. But she couldn't blame Wonsang. After all, those things would have bothered anyone. It was perfectly understandable when she thought about how they'd had to evict the tenants downstairs so that Jungeon and Sunil could move in. They'd needed to return the 80 million won deposit to the tenants, and Jungeon and Sunil hadn't possessed even half of that amount. Wonsang had come up with the rest of the money without a word of complaint and never mentioned it again. Yeongjin didn't know anyone else who would do something like that. And was it two years ago in the fall? Yeongjin recalled their trip to Jeju Island. She and Wonsang, the kids, and her side of the family, minus Mansu, had all gone on the trip. Wonsang rented a nine-passenger van and did the driving. If sales was Yeongjin's gift, driving was Wonsang's. He drove smoothly and confidently. As they made their way from Jeju City to Seongsan Ilchulbong Peak and then to Seogwipo, they stopped at a low volcanic cone. The cone was covered with silver grass, making it difficult to move through. The wind whipped the grass, turning it silvery one moment and gray the next. From the bottom of the knoll, the grass looked like waves or a giant furry beast hunched over, taking a nap. Sunil wanted to go to the top, but her knees were bad, and all she could do was pace back and forth, staring at the grass. Wonsang crouched down and offered to carry her on his back, and she climbed on. Yeongjin saw it the moment it happened. If she'd looked a second later, she would have missed it. He's so big and my mom's so small, she thought, watching them, somewhat shocked. Wonsang started to climb the knoll with Sunil on his back. He was someone who could do something like that, matter-of-factly, without fanfare. Without too much thought or boasting.

Of course, there were times she felt let down and anxious, but she didn't believe Wonsang was a bad person. He just didn't . . . think enough. That's what she believed. To Yeongjin, thinking was a kind of desperation. Just because you have a thought doesn't mean you should say it or act on it. And just because you want to say or do something doesn't mean you should actually say it or do it. You should hold it in. You should bear it. Wonsang simply did this less, just like any ordinary person. It's what most people did, every single day.

Yeongjin grabbed the two corners of the comforter she'd brought out to show a customer and stretched out her arms to fold it back up again. The sound of the fabric brushing against itself was soothing. New comforters, new fabric. She liked the smell of new comforters, unused by anyone. What would you call this smell that had no odor? If there ever was a large bird that would come into this world without hatching from an egg, a bird that wouldn't eat or sleep and would live only for ten minutes and then vanish, she believed its wings would smell like this. A comforter that had been used by someone for even one night didn't smell the same. There were customers who brought back their comforters, claiming they were unused. She issued returns to most of them, but not because she believed their lies. From the very start, she knew they were lying. She knew how shameless people could be, how they could lie while looking you straight in the eye.

Yeongjin put the comforter back in its place and faced the counter. She spread open one of the picture books beside the card machine. Since the books contained only pictures, she had thought her kids would find them dull, but maybe they wouldn't. Perhaps they would enjoy them, making up their own stories by looking at the illustrations. Each child might come up with a completely different story. Her firstborn was seven and her second was five. She liked these ages. The children ran and played and were honest for the most part. When she told them to be quiet, they listened, and they were mature for their age, too. She'd been told this was because she'd had them later in life. Once when she'd taken the children to the pediatrician, an elderly woman who'd brought her grandson had told her so. The woman kept looking at Yeongjin and asked if she was their mother. She then asked how old Yeongjin was, and said it all made sense now. She'd been wondering how such young kids could sit still. All this she said as if it were a compliment.

After Yeongjin had children, she learned that contrary to what the world said, the maternal instinct didn't come naturally. When she'd been pregnant with her first, her mother-in-law mentioned *geriatric pregnancy* habitually, bemoaning Yeongjin's physical condition and worrying about the health of the baby. As soon as the baby was born, she came to the hospital and wept. In gestures that seemed overly conscious of her father-in-law, Wonsang, and even the nurse who showed them the baby through the window, her mother-in-law wiped away tears and stretched her hand toward the window, saying, Oh, my baby, my little baby. To Yeongjin, who'd been in labor for over thirty hours and was now sitting in a wheelchair after being sewn back up, her mother-in-law's actions seemed bizarre. Why are you crying? Why all this fuss over a baby you're seeing for the first time? Every second,

Yeongjin had suppressed her rage. She hated everyone, the other mothers and their caregivers in the hospital room with her, the nurses, the doctors, Wonsang, her father-in-law, her mother-in-law, her side of the family who had quietly come and gone, as if walking on eggshells. All she wanted to do was wash her body that reeked of blood, her filthy body that was naked under the thin hospital gown. In the middle of the night when she was dead asleep and the nurse shook her awake to send her to the nursing room and put the baby to her breast, she felt shame. The baby felt like a stranger. She wanted to scream and ask if they had mixed up the babies by accident, if they were sure this baby was hers. Whenever the baby couldn't latch properly and would shriek and turn red and the nurses would offer advice as if it were the mother's fault, Yeongjin felt despair and rage and guilt. Everything was horrific, but the baby, the baby in her arms was the most horrific of all. Its blindness, its weakness, its tenacity. This stranger who'd come to take over her life, who demanded everything of her. Yeongjin tried desperately to hide her thoughts and emotions. She believed something was wrong with her, that she was defective for lacking the maternal instinct, and instead of heading to a postpartum care center, she went straight home. She was scared to be around other mothers. Since Yeobum's birthday is in the fall . . . Yes, it had been fall. That fall, she stayed home with her newborn. With her ruined body that would not heal, she was left alone with the baby.

One day she came to her senses to find an elderly woman peering into her face. Mama, are you okay? The woman said she'd heard a baby crying nonstop, so she'd followed the sound and found the apartment door unlocked and Yeongjin lying in bed like this. Yeongjin tried to get up, but couldn't. All she could do was weep, and while she continued to weep, the stranger held and soothed the baby, singing what sounded like a lullaby, or hymn, Yeongjin wasn't sure. Judging from the sign of the cross she kept making, she seemed to be Catholic. After she left, Yeongjin called Sunil. Mom, Mom. After hearing what had happened, Sunil came to Yeongjin's house.

At first, Sunil brought just one suitcase, and around the time Yeongjin was about to have the second baby, Sunil brought her kitchen utensils. Using these things, she fed Yeongjin and Yeongjin's children and looked after them. Yeongjin wondered how long ago that had been. How many years has it been and what year was it now.

She was able to bond with the baby after the newborn stage. The feeling of missing him, the wonder and excitement of seeing him make a new expression or gesture, pitying and loving his scrunched face, feeling generous and patient toward him . . . All these things came with time. She thought there needed to be a more suitable word to describe her maternal instinct, for hers wasn't innate, but learned and developed through time and interaction. It was something that needed to be formed. Because she knew this, she'd been able to have a second child and accept it with ease, more than she had with her first. She loved her children now. Yeongjin knew Sunil had made it possible. Sunil's labors had made everything possible.

Yet, the night before, Yeongjin had heard Sunil's story. Sunil had said she was tired. All day she'd been so tired she'd kept dozing off. That she'd done the housework while dozing off.

Yeongjin was listening, not because she wanted to, and not because her mom seemed nervous and desperate. It was because she was so tired that she couldn't get up from the table. Sunil complained about how she'd phoned Sejin and told her to come pick up the banchan she'd made, but the girl wouldn't come. She grumbled about how picky an eater Jungeon was, wanting meat or fish with every meal, and how every time she phoned Mansu her calls kept getting dropped. Your dad keeps telling me to ask Mansu when he's going to come home, but how's he supposed to do that when he needs to pay an arm and a leg for flights . . . Yeongjin nodded, thinking her dad was slowly getting the hint. Jungeon expected Mansu to come home, but Yeongjin didn't think Mansu had any plans to return. In her opinion, it would be a bigger headache if he wanted to come back. Jungeon believed a family should stay together, but Sunil didn't know what the boy could do in Korea, so it was better for him to stay put. New Zealand was a better place to live. Yeongjin nodded along, half-listening to Sunil.

She didn't know when the story started. By the time she realized, Sunil was already deep into it. While Sunil talked, Yeongjin thought about the rumors she and her friends had heard in high school. All the rumors, the bizarre tales about the hospital Sunil had just mentioned. The hospital was near the end of a bus route by their school and was notorious for abortions. A place more women went to get rid of their babies than to have them. Kids called the hospital *red light* and said the whole area was filthy, sharing all kinds of gossip. For example, they claimed that because of the blood of so many dead babies, there was a strange smell whenever you turned on the tap, and if you even went near the hospital . . . From the moment Sunil mentioned the hospital name, Yeongjin thought of everything she and her friends had said about the women who went there.

Twice.

Sunil said she'd gone there twice. Once before Yeongjin was born and once after.

Yeongjin knew she was staring too intently at her mom's face, but she couldn't look away. Sunil was sitting at the table across from her.

She felt as if she were looking at Sunil's naked body. A body different from the one she'd seen countless times as a child, at the public bath or at home. Sunil shut her eyes and lifted the hem of her apron to dab at her tears. Yeongjin closed her eyes. Red light, red light . . . Mom, Mom, Yeongjin said. All right, go to bed.

It's late.

•

Now Yeongjin was worried about what she'd said. She thought about her tone, about her mom's expression that night. Sunil had stayed silent. She'd only nodded, saying nothing.

When Yeongjin remembered how Sunil had gone downstairs to sleep without saying another word, she felt as if a heavy sack were pressing down on her, sinking toward the pit of her stomach. Mom's body . . . I thought I knew all there was to know about her body, that I'd figured it all out, but how could her mom's words right then have been so horrific?

All right, go to bed.

It's late.

Her mom had never told anyone. Yeongjin knew as soon as Sunil started talking about it. The unspoken story had now come to Yeongjin. Thinking about it kept making her mind go blank. Why on earth would Mom tell me something like that?

Yeongjin remembered the meals that had been spread out on the living room table of her childhood home. Any time Sunil was home, she would go back and forth between the kitchen and living room, wearing an apron that covered her chest and stomach. Not a lightweight apron made of linen, but the kind that market vendors wore that was waterproof and effective against contamination. In that apron, her mom seemed more like a butcher than a housewife. She'd probably had to wear something like that because there was always an endless list of things to do in that house. In that apron . . . To fill the bellies of her family, her mom bought large hunks of meat or cheap beef bones, soaking them in water for hours to take the blood out, and made shockingly delicious broth. But there was always too much food, always too much soup and banchan, and the smell was on the people from this house, it had seeped into their skin, into their pores. Children who smelled of grilled fish and chili oil. Yeongjin was the first of these children to become an adult and get a job.

Every night under the streetlight in front of their house, Sunil waited for Yeongjin. When Yeongjin turned the dark corner and saw her mom standing under the distant light, she felt as if she'd start crying. To hide her emotions, she'd step into the house grumbling, and there would be her dinner on the living room table—freshly made rice and soup. Every night, Yeongjin ate her dinner while nodding off, and if she happened to receive her paycheck that day, she carefully set down the envelope, as if adhering it to the surface. All while swallowing the pride and scorn and resentment and rage toward that table.

No matter how late I'd come home, my mom always waited up for me.

Yeongjin would say things like this to her co-workers while drinking, and begin to cry. She'd always start by saying, My mom and I have a special bond.

No matter how late I got off work, she'd leave the kitchen light on and wait for me. Everyone would be asleep, but not her. Every night, she'd have dinner ready, freshly made rice and soup.

But Mom, why aren't you like this with Mansu?

Why do you say he can live there, but you never said that to me? Why do you say he doesn't have to come back? That he should stay where he wants to stay?

I've always wanted to ask you that.

You can't do everything you want in life.

Yeongjin had heard this a long time ago, and whenever she had to make an important decision, these words served as a guideline. She believed it had been the same for Sunil. With time, she realized this was the ultimate truth. A path to a wiser, less miserable truth. Because you can't do everything you want in life.

Yeongjin tried to recall who'd said these words or where she'd heard them, but she couldn't remember. Who was it—Mom, Father, my teachers, my elders?

Do you have anything softer?

A customer walked into the store, fingering each comforter in her path. Something good for eczema? My kids have severe eczema . . . After staring intently at the customer's face, Yeongjin led her to the section with the most suitable comforters. This customer would be her last for the day. The PA announced that the department store would be closing soon.

•

Yeongjin buttoned up her coat and flipped open her cell phone to check for new messages. There were several texts from Wonsang. When she hadn't responded to his texts in the morning, it seemed he was trying to gauge her mood. She imagined what kind of words they would exchange at home. She didn't feel like talking to Wonsang. At least not today. He'd ask if she was angry. If she was angry again. She pulled the purse strap that had slipped off her shoulder back into place and headed toward the subway station. After watching the train pull into the station, the doors open, and the passengers get off, she climbed aboard. Tonight, she was more worried about facing her mom than her husband. There were things Yeongjin wanted to say, things she'd wanted to ask Sunil for a long time. Why have you kept me here? Why do you insist on keeping me at your table? But she didn't have the courage to ask. She lacked the courage to look at Sunil's face after asking, or to wait for Sunil to respond. Sunil was now in her seventies, her body worn down from having looked after people all her life. The moment when Yeongjin could finally ask her might never come. If she did, her mom might cry, and she didn't want to see her cry.

You can't do everything you want in life.

Yeongjin had heard these words spoken by a voice from her memory, or perhaps not. Had it been someone on the train just now? Yeongjin turned to see who it could have been.

The train emerged aboveground and began to cross the railroad bridge.

•

Lies.

•

Lies. Yeongjin had no idea why she tasted blood every time this word came to mind.

nameless

Yi Sunil once sailed through the air and plunged into the snow.

She'd been a child, about three or four years old. Stunned, she lay looking up at the night sky. Several stars glittered above, so bright they looked as if they might shatter. Her eyes and mouth were full of snow. Some had gone inside her mouth, and it dissolved right away, trickling down her throat. Out of everything she's ever tasted, the only thing that tasted similar was cotton muslin. Muslin, cool against the skin. Nets woven with white thread. It was her mother who pulled her out of the snow. At least that's what she believed. Because why would it have been anyone else?

Her mother scolded someone, saying, Why would you throw her like that?

Because she's running around at night, that's why, a man said.

Someone stood at the edge of the living room floor, the light shining behind him. It was probably her father. Because why would it have been anyone else?

•

When Sunja asked Sunil if she looked like her mother or her father, what came to mind was that particular memory. That night, free-falling through the air, the pile of snow cushioning her narrow back, fingers digging under her arms. She couldn't recall any faces. Those two people had disappeared from her life much too early. Her father had been made the chairman of the village committee under the People's Army, but when the front line between North and South Korea kept shifting, he'd gone missing. He was told he would live if he turned himself in, so he went to the South Korean army to surrender, but he never came back. Sunil had no idea how he died or why he wasn't able to return, but she heard how her mother died.

A disease spread around the village. A neighbor who'd caught it was too sick to draw water, so they asked your mother to go fetch some water for them. Your mother couldn't say no, and she ended up catching it when she carried the water into the infected house.

It was before the North Korean soldiers came. Sunil recalled sleeping and eating in a room with only kids for several days. Then one day, her father's elder brother came and called her out to the courtyard, saying he was going to take her to see her mother. She went with him, but when they arrived at their destination, Sunil found herself in a big house she'd never seen before. Paper-covered doors, removed to connect the different rooms, were stored and fastened near the rafters. So many rooms. Sunil wandered through each one, peering at everything. She didn't know if it had been a dream or hallucination, but all the rooms were empty, and because of the air drifting through the open space, the wooden floor was cold. Exhausted, she'd been looking out from one of these rooms when an old man with a long, coarse beard stopped in the middle of the courtyard and asked, Hey kid, where'd your mother go? He then burst into laughter. The inside of his mouth was black. She remembered the old man, the courtyard. She told Sunja her mother had probably died that day.

You must have been so sad, Sunja said.

Sunil said she wasn't.

I was just a kid, so I didn't know any better . . .

She wasn't sad, and it was only when she got older that she felt that way. This conversation had started, all because Sunja had asked Sunil for her mother's name.

When Sejin told Sunil she was going to Germany, Sunil told her to visit Sunja.

When you get there, go see her. Look her up.

Sejin stared at her, blinking in confusion. Who?

Sunja.

Who's that?

You don't know Sunja?

Who's Sunja?

You really don't know who she is?

Confused, Sunil gazed at her daughter. To think her daughter didn't know who Sunja was. Sunja, who'd lost her parents in Galgol, Toseong-ri village, in the town of Galmal in Cheorwon County. Sunja, who'd lived after that with Grandfather in Jigyeong-ri village. And then when this Sunja was fifteen, she had met another Sunja in Songjeong-ri village, Yangseo of Gimpo County, Gyeonggi Province. Her friend, neighbor, and peer, who had the same name as her. Even when she'd slapped Sunja in the face, she had not cried. How was she supposed to tell Sejin all this? Where was she supposed to start? Not knowing what to say, Sunil could only stare back at her daughter.

And she lives in Germany?

Sunil was about to say yes, but realized this wasn't true. Sunil hadn't spoken to Sunja again after 1967. After the fire that burned down part of Songjeong Market and several houses nearby, she hadn't seen Sunja, not even once. Despite it all, she'd believed Sunja was still in Germany. She moved to Germany and she's there still, she'd told herself. It was all so real to Sunil, as if she'd actually seen and heard so herself. Sunja glancing back in a dress suit, stockings, and heels, with a small Korean flag sewn over her left breast, and her hair tied back in preparation for the long-distance flight. Sunja, who had aged gracefully, sitting against a white wall, laughing, dressed in a solid-color knit shirt and her graying hair in a short bob. It was the strangest thing. How could Sunja's past and present be so clear in Sunil's mind when she hadn't actually seen any of it?

Hey kid, where'd your mother go?

Scenes so vivid they seemed less real the more she thought of them. Then whose, she wondered, whose memories were they?

·

Sunil put the wet laundry in the basket and went up to the rooftop. She hung up Yeongjin's blouse, Wonsang's T-shirt, and Jungeon's dress shirt, and clipped the children's pants and tights in place. The clothesline sagged from the weight. She adjusted the pole to make the line taut and stepped back. The smell of the clean laundry was refreshing. Breathing it in, she looked toward the hillside about one hundred fifty meters south.

The hill, now cleanly cut with its underside exposed, towered into the sky like a colossal wall. It looked like a gigantic wave that was about to swallow her up. She heard the grating of the excavator, scraping at the broken fragments of the demolished houses. Though she couldn't see, the noise seemed to be coming from the other side of the hill. This side had been completed last week. Homes with umbrellas, shoe racks, and household appliances spilling out onto the balcony, old run-down houses with attic windows peeping out from under sloping roofs with faded tiles, neglected homes with peeling paint and cracks running along the walls—they had covered the entire hillside, but they were all gone now. Apartment construction was in progress with completion planned for next year. Sunil didn't think it was a good idea for a cluster of high-rises to be built on a slope. Will the land be able to bear the weight of the buildings? Whenever she looked at the hill, she couldn't help thinking of the apartment building on the Wawoo Mountain slope that had collapsed overnight.

That year, in the spring of 1970, she had been at the market selling produce out of a basket next to a dried fish store. Business was good. The market was thriving back then. On many days, she was so busy that she got by with eating whatever was within reach. It was from that point Sunil began to eat tomatoes regularly. If she felt hungry, thirsty, or light-headed while working, she reached for a tomato. Just one was enough to stave off her hunger and thirst. She rarely caught colds or became ill, and her eyesight was good compared to others her age. She believed the tomatoes were the reason. She constantly pushed them on her children, but they didn't like tomatoes. In fact, they hated them, saying they made their lips swell. Sunil knew tomatoes contained toxins. But wasn't it only natural for something so potent to contain toxins?

She also grew tomatoes in her garden. Each year, she obtained new seedlings and planted them. The garden belonged to her, and the entire family even referred to it as "Mom's garden." After all, she'd built it herself. She'd made the border with bricks and cinder blocks, laid out several layers of tarp for the lining, brought in soil she'd gathered from various places, and filled the bed with flowers and plants. The garden, which had started out a few years ago as a one-by-one-meter bed, had now expanded to about 3 x 1.5 meters. This summer, again, tomatoes of all different sizes grew.

She'd also grown flowers in pots until the previous year, but after her son-in-law's niece and nephews came for a visit and ripped all the leaves and petals to pieces, she transferred the soil into the garden bed and emptied the pots, leaving them upside-down. Rose moss, zinnias, hollyhocks, cleomes. After the kids tore through the garden, she found the ground littered with blossoms and naked stems standing in the pots and garden bed. Though the kids' parents, and even Sunil's own children, viewed the unfortunate incident as typical behavior for children, Sunil didn't touch the housework for four days afterward. What they had done was unforgivable. A fistful of chrysanthemums and some balloon vines had been all that remained.

Sunil picked a red, ripe tomato and held it in her hand. It felt almost hot, having soaked up the sun.

If only I could get my hands on some good soil, she thought, holding the tomato. But how? It was difficult enough to get any kind of soil, let alone good soil.

Each time she found herself wishing for some good soil, she thought about the fields of Toseong-ri and Jigyeong-ri in Cheorwon County. Fluffy levees of dark, rich earth. Everything grew well in that earth. Radishes, cabbage, you name it. Whenever Sunil longed for those fields and the crops grown in those fields, her daughters suggested that she pack up her life in the city and move back. It was a ridiculous suggestion. She had no such desire. It's not that she missed the place. Her husband, who was originally from north of the 38th parallel, sometimes went to Imjingak to gaze out toward his hometown, but Sunil didn't feel any need to do that. There was nothing she missed about what others would call her hometown. For as long as she could remember and even now, only the elderly lived there. She pictured the faces of the old people she knew. People who were neither wise nor kind. Maybe that's just what happens when you get old, she thought, poking through the dark green stalks. I'm old now, too. She picked several more tomatoes, put them in her apron pocket, and headed downstairs.

Yeongjin was sitting at the table, half-awake. Her hair and face were dry. It seemed she hadn't washed up yet. Sunil pulled out the tomatoes and placed them on the counter. You want some breakfast?

Yeongjin shook her head.

How about some tomatoes?

She scrubbed them in running water, placed them on the chopping board, and quickly sliced them up. After plating them and sprinkling a bit of sugar on top, she set the plate down before Yeongjin.

Mom, you know they make my lips swell, Yeongjin said. They make my lips burn.

Still, she pierced a slice with her fork and put it in her mouth and chewed. She looked as if she had a toothache. That child always makes that kind of face whenever she eats something, Sunil thought. She recalled what Yeongjin had said to her several days before. She'd asked why Sunil had taken them. But Sunil knew Yeongjin hadn't expected an answer. Sunil held the chopping board under the tap and watched the stream wash away the runny seeds.

Mom, Yeongjin said in a raspy voice. Can you give me some water?

Sunja.

That was what people in the villages of Toseong-ri and Jigyeong-ri had called Sunil.

Come here, Sunja.

Sunja, that little hussy.

That Sunja.

The adults who had called her by that name were now all dead, or nearly dead. Her uncle, her father's eldest brother, who had defected to North Korea the year the Korean War broke out, must have died by now, but his wife, who'd been very young at the time, was most likely still alive. She'd been his second wife. She had cooked for Sunil, who had been entrusted into her uncle's care. Sunil recalled the wife's flat little knot of hair held in place with a black hairpin that resembled a long metal nail, how she would peer into the hearth or stir the porridge with a wooden spoon, wearing a plain traditional jacket and wrinkled skirt. Sunil recalled worrying that the big hairpin would fall into the pot. At the time, she had believed the hairpin was too big, but when she became an adult, she realized it was the knot of hair that was too small, smaller than a child's fist. Sometimes at night, the wife pinched Sunil's leg with her toes, making Sunil jump in pain and shock. She'd glance around to see the wife's face and the whites of her eyes gleaming in the dark, looking at her. But no matter what time of day, she found something odd and creepy about that face. The wife was twelve, maybe thirteen years old at most. When Sunil would consider the ridiculous things her own children did at that age, the saying "time is fair to everyone"—now where had she heard that?—would come to mind. She's been thinking of it more and more as of late. It didn't make any sense.

Where was her uncle's wife from? she wondered much later. She'd used a kind of southern dialect. Where was her home? The elders said she was from a dead-broke family. When Sunil heard that as a child, she'd been appalled. What was dead and broken? Each time Sunil looked at the wife's face, those words came to mind, and she didn't like it. Or maybe she was just scared. A girl hiding what was dead and broken under her blouse and skirt.

Sunil's uncle, who had brought her to be his second wife, worked on a railway-related project with the Japanese who had moved to the nearby village of Jipo-ri. He made his money working in their office. But when the North Korean People's Army crossed the mountain and entered Galgol, he became concerned about his connection to the Japanese and paid an urgent visit to his younger brother, accompanied by members of the village committee.

You might not be educated, but you're smart, they said to Sunil's father, urging him to take over as chairman of the village committee. It was her uncle who had encouraged him to serve in this new role, saying it would benefit the rest of the family. This is what Sunil heard much later, when the older people were talking among themselves. They clucked their tongues, saying, That's what happens when things are a mess and you can't keep your wits about you.

They said that when the UN forces recaptured the Galgol area, it was her uncle who again urged her father to surrender. When her father went to the South Korean army to turn himself in and was never heard from again, her uncle got scared and decided to defect to North Korea.

Sunil recalled that night.

A cabbage field. There were others, besides her uncle and his young wife. Adults. She did as they did, crawling on hands and knees along the frost-covered furrows. Because the levees were high, the furrows were deep. She cut her hands and chin on the frozen dirt, sharp as razorblades, but she was hardly aware of the pain. She was terrified of being left behind. Though she struggled to crawl after them, she fell back. While in this panic, the sky suddenly turned white, as if from lightening or a flare, and the adults ahead lay flat on the ground. She, too, flattened herself like them, her forehead against the cold, damp earth, but when she looked up again, they were gone.

They had disappeared.

Sunil clamped her mouth shut and thought about that night. After sitting in the moonlight between the cabbages for some time, she retraced her steps and returned to her uncle's house. She rummaged through the kitchen and ate whatever she could find and stayed in that empty house for several days. One night, two nights, three nights. And then, at last, she was discovered by the villagers and was sent south to the village of Jigyeong-ri to live with her mother's father, who had resolved to remain and die in his home, because he lacked the energy to flee.

Sunil had one picture of Grandfather. She hung it near the top of the wall, surrounded by family photos that multiplied every year. Her wedding photo, Yeongjin's first birthday, Mansu's first birthday, Yeongjin's first day of elementary school, Sejin's middle school graduation, Yeongjin's high school graduation, Mansu's first day of university. As the pictures multiplied, her grandfather's face became more unfamiliar. Yeongjin or Mansu had said she resembled her grandfather, but she didn't see the resemblance at all. She had never liked him. The short, old man had a nasty temper. He shouted often, he let his grizzly, curly beard grow thick and unkempt, and the front of his shirt and pants always reeked of sour rice wine. He felt no shame about his grimy leggings and collar, and he was illiterate and stubborn. When he fled Jigyeong-ri during the war to stay in Suwon, he took Sunil with him, but he often let his granddaughter go hungry while he ate. Once the war was over and they returned to Jigyeong-ri, he put a yoke on Sunil's shoulders or tied it around her waist, making her drag the plow, which he held while following from behind. He made her work the field this way. If she sought refuge at school to avoid that hard, hateful labor, he'd come to the school, clutching a rod, with an A-frame on his back, calling for her as if he had some urgent business.

Hey, Sunja.

Hey.

Your grandfather's here.

Her classmates would tell her, and her face would flush in shame, and she would have no choice but to follow him home. At night if she kept the oil lamp burning because she was reading and writing, he rubbed the wick between his thumb and forefinger and snuffed out the flame. The old man, usually a man of few words, became talkative when he drank. He'd point at her and say she was the only one left.

Everyone died and she's the only one left. The only one alive.

She hated it whenever he said that. She couldn't forgive him. Because there had been not one, but two granddaughters entrusted to him.

Sunil believed if she had crawled along the cabbage field on her own, she wouldn't have lost sight of the adults. If she had been alone, she would have been able to crawl quickly enough to keep up with them. But my little sister had been with me. She was tied to my back, like a small sack of onions. Every time I crawled forward by pushing off the ground and sticking my bottom in the air, my sister's head rattled and mashed against the back of my neck. A three-year-old's weight on a five-year-old's back. That night in the field, I learned what a ton of bricks felt like. When I went back to my uncle's house, she was still on my back. When I went into the yard and stood for a long time with my back to the moon, when I lay waiting for dawn in the ransacked room, littered with signs of frantic packing, she was still there. Then a few days later when I was discovered by the village adults, she was still there, and when I pushed open the straw gate of the Jigyeong-ri house and saw Grandfather, when I had my first meal there—a boiled potato with some dongchimi kimchi—on a small scratched-up table with cabriole legs, she was still there.

In the winter, communist troops came from China. They wore balaclava hats and belted overcoats with cotton padding, and remained in the village for some time. They carried out their orders and ate voraciously. They searched every home, slaughtering and eating the villagers' livestock and seizing their grain and cauldrons. The whole village, including Grandfather, scorned the soldiers for their ignorance, for making rice in a cauldron reserved for boiling cow fodder, for storing food in a crock used to ferment urine to make fertilizer, but when summoned, they went to help without a single complaint. And on the day when Grandfather briefly left the house to help the soldiers, and Sunil was crouching in front of the fire stove to warm herself, her little sister was still there.

The stove was already lit under the cauldron for dinner. Sunil dozed off, her face and shoulders warmed by the fire. She remembered her sister's padded skirt, spread in the shape of a small bell over the ash-covered dirt floor. She cried for Mom, and I prodded the fire with the poker. In the process, a burning twig was dragged out onto the kitchen floor, transferring the fire onto the hem of my sister's skirt. An ember that popped out could have been the cause, but Sunil believed it was the burning twig that spread the fire to the child's skirt. That's how she remembered it. The cotton padding in the skirt swallowed up the spark and burned red, while black flames darted up, devouring the outer fabric. Her sister ran out into the yard and started rolling in the dirt, but the fire didn't go out. When Sunil beat the fire with the poker, the jacket and skirt seemed to flap harder, making the clothes burn faster. Sunil, completely helpless, was shrieking when her grandfather returned. At that point, the burning fabric clung to her sister's skin, scorching her flesh. Sunil's grandfather ran to the child, putting out the fire by frantically beating and rubbing at the flames with his bare hands, but it was too late. The child lay on the cold floor for three days and then died.

It took three days.

At times Sunil wondered if she'd ever had a sister, but she never completely forgot those three days. There was nothing to do, nothing she could do. She did as her grandfather instructed and grated potatoes and covered her sister's body with the paste. The paste absorbed her sister's blood and pus, turning from maroon to brown, and finally hardening into a black scab. All day and night, she watched her sister lying on the cold floor and waited for her breathing to stop.

That smell, that sound.

Her grandfather suffered burns on his hands, which became deformed and covered with keloid scars, and his fingernails fell off. The thumb and index finger on his left hand, the index and middle fingers on his right. He never blamed her for that, nor for her sister's death. He never even mentioned the incident. But every time he said she was the only one left, she believed he was referring to that day. Because she had beaten the burning cotton, inadvertently spreading the fire over her sister's body. He didn't say so, but Sunil felt as if she'd heard those words. She believed he didn't mention the incident because he couldn't forgive her.

The only one alive.

So when her aunt came to get her, claiming to be her father's half-sister, Sunil had no reason not to go with her. She followed this aunt to Songjeong-ri village, Gimpo County. It was the summer of 1960, the year Sunil turned fifteen.

•

As Sunil was washing the pan she'd left in the sink the night before, she remembered the leftover batter for zucchini fritters that she'd forgotten to refrigerate. When she lifted the paper towel that was covering the plastic bowl, she noticed a bit of water had pooled on top, but the batter seemed fine otherwise. It hadn't spoiled. With the day being a holiday and everyone likely to sleep in, she decided to make the fritters for lunch. The fridge on the fifth floor was full, so she took the batter down to the fourth floor. Sejin, who was brushing her teeth, stuck her head out of the bathroom.

Is Eonni up?

No, she went back to bed.

Even after an argument, she still asks about her big sister, Sunil thought. She heard Sejin turn on the tap and rinse her mouth.

You're leaving now?

No, later. When did Dad head out?

At dawn.

But it's his birthday today.

That makes no difference for security guards. These days, he leaves at five in the morning.

Sejin and Yeongjin had argued the night before. Everything had been fine when they started with the bottle of wine Sejin had brought, followed by the hard liquor Wonsang fetched from the balcony. However, the mood shifted after Jungeon went downstairs to sleep and a flushed Wonsang called it a night. Yeongjin kept badgering Sejin about her work, whether she was making any money, and if so, how much— questions Sejin managed to deflect until Yeongjin finally asked how long she planned to live this way. If you're going to keep this up, come work for me instead.

No.

Why not?

I can't.

Why not?

I'm not good at that.

No one's good at first. Everyone starts somewhere.

But I don't want to do that.

Sejin, Yeongjin said. You can't do everything you want in life. You think people only do what they want to do?

Sunil heard what Yeongjin said and saw Sejin's face turn cold. The effort to be accommodating vanished as Sejin assumed an expression the whole family recognized. Her forehead turned smooth, her eyes narrowed, and her mouth clamped shut. Yeongjin, too, closed her mouth. Everyone knew this expression as well. A face that declared a situation impossible, the matter closed. The argument ended this way. When they were young, Sunil thought. When these kids had been young, she could intervene. She could scold one or both, placate them or mediate disputes, but that was no longer possible. Their conflicts were less frequent now, yet when they did occur, they were about matters much harsher and more personal. Whatever the issue was, Sunil felt a pang of remorse. She felt she had been the one to pass it on to the kids, and once in their hands, it had shattered into pieces, making their hands bleed.

Sunil put the batter in the fridge, took off her apron, and went into her room. She and Jungeon had been using separate rooms for a long time. Her room was filled with clothes, blankets, and cabinets for dishes and small appliances, while Jungeon's was filled with an electric bed, desk, swivel chair, bookshelf, and documents. Somewhere in his room was probably the Galgol document—the title deed for the mountain that had belonged to Sunil's father, which she'd registered in Jungeon's name. Sunil wasn't interested in the document's value, for she knew where the mountain was located. In the fall, the ground would be covered with a thick carpet of brown pine needles, and chestnuts would fall and sink into the cushiony slope. Many chestnut trees grew on that mountain, but their family couldn't harvest a single one. In order for the mountain to be of any use to the children, there first had to be a reunification of North and South Korea, or some sort of inter-Korean exchange, but Jungeon didn't seem to be hoping for that. How could he possibly get along with the Reds he said he knew so well? Sunil picked up her wallet from her vanity, made sure her debit card and cash were inside, and put it in her pocket. She rummaged through the shelves for her sunhat and walked deeper into the room, finding it on her bed, which was at the far end of the room.

Leaving a passage just wide enough for one person to walk through, Sunil brought various drawers, wardrobes, and shelves into the room, creating a labyrinth. She had to round two corners, following the narrow passage shaped like the character ⊏, to reach the single bed at the end. On both sides of the passage leading to the bed were glass cabinets holding stacks of out-of-season clothes for every family member, including her adult children who'd moved out. The different colors in the cross-section of the clothes made the room resemble the rock strata of a canyon. Due to the sheer number of objects filling the space, no one dared set foot in there, and for this Sunil was glad. When she lay on her bed at the end of the labyrinth, she could see the sky through the curtainless window. There, Sunil was alone and at peace. However, it was also in this room that items frequently went missing. Whenever she acquired something nice, she'd place it nearby, intending to save it for later, but she often forgot where she put it. She would say she had been too careful each time this happened. Even if she never found it again, she wasn't too upset or worried. After all, it wasn't gone or lost. It was simply forgotten, which meant it was still there, somewhere.

What's all this?

Whenever Mansu returned to Korea, he was aghast at the state of their apartment. He stared, stunned, at the objects that filled Sunil's room, kitchen, and balcony. Mom, you've got to throw things out. You really have to. He looked stricken, as if he'd witnessed signs or symptoms of something much more serious than a mere pile of objects. Sunil knew he secretly discarded some items each time he returned home, but she didn't care. She couldn't tell what was missing. Forgotten, not lost. They were still there, somewhere.

When Sunil stepped out of her room wearing a hat, Sejin asked where she was going.

I'll be right back.

Where are you going?

Using her cane, Sunil treaded down the stairs with care, with Sejin following from behind. Mom, if you feel like you're going to fall, just fall back, I'm right behind you.

Sunil made her way down ever so slowly, and when she finally stepped outside, the sun still blinded her, despite her hat. She headed toward the public market with Sejin, who walked next to her. She rounded the corner of a grocery store with a wide awning facing the road. They entered a covered arcade that sloped gently down for about five hundred meters. The market had decent fruit and fish, though the meat wasn't as good, and the vegetables were sometimes good, sometimes not. However, the best thing about this market was its bustling atmosphere. Even on a regular weekday, the aisles teemed with people shopping and browsing, both at lunch and dinner, and the voices of the merchants calling out to customers were full of energy. Sunil bought two sugar twists at a stall where donuts, looking like plump skeins, had been fried to a golden brown, and handed one to Sejin. Grease soaked through the parchment wrappers and onto their fingers. They passed a mill while eating their twists and Sunil remembered her sesame seeds, which she'd stored in her pantry. Kim Geunil, her old neighbor from Cheorwon, had sent her a sack containing about five liters of perilla seeds. She needed to take them to a mill to make perilla oil, but she didn't trust the mills in this neighborhood. She didn't want to take dried chili peppers, seeds, or good-quality grain anywhere else other than the old mill in the Gangseo District in Seoul. She believed the old mill was still in business, but she wasn't sure. The last time she'd gone there was three years ago. High shelves had been added to the front of the mill and they'd been filled with seedling pots. The owner said not as many people came in to press oil anymore and that he now made a living mostly by selling seedlings. They were popular, but he didn't understand why people bought them. Did they even have a place to grow them? This is what the owner had said three years ago. She didn't know if the situation was still the same.

The market in Gonghang-dong was in decline then. It was there that Sunil spent her teens, ran a business after getting married in her twenties, practically fled after going bankrupt in her forties, and continued to visit well into her sixties. Many of the stalls stood empty, and though some stores remained open, there were hardly any merchants or customers. Without them, the market aged. The only thing left for the dying market, situated on a slope leading down to the cattle yard, was to go to ruin. Most of the merchants, including Sunil and Jungeon, who had supported each other over the years but had also been entangled in the embezzlement incident, had since left. The produce store, the fish store, the dried fish store, the drapery store, the toy store, and the fast-food joint had all closed and the only business that stayed open was the stall that sold soondae sausages. The store had thick plastic sheeting for walls, a brazier where the sausages were boiled, and two stools for customers. Inside, the now-elderly woman dozed, sitting on a third stool filled with coal briquettes and a blanket pulled up to her neck. Sunil recalled the woman's face from years ago. Do you remember me, Sunil asked her. The old woman blinked, looking embarrassed, and then sliced up a sausage. She pushed the pieces to one side of the chopping board and gestured for her to eat. It seemed she could hardly hear.

Granny, can I help you find anything?

A man called out to Sunil, dusting the shoes on display with a wool duster. Sunil glanced up from the children's patent leather shoes she'd been eyeing. She said she was looking for hiking boots.

His eyes darted to her cane. For yourself?

What would I do with hiking boots? For my daughter, not me.

He jutted his chin toward Sejin, who was wiping the grease from her mouth with the back of her hand.

Her?

No, a different daughter. I have another daughter.

You should be looking in the women's section then.

He shook his duster and told them to come inside.

Sunja.

If you come and stay with me for a couple of years, I'll make sure you get an education and learn a trade like you always wanted, I'll feed you and clothe you with nice things, better than what you get out here, and when the time comes, I'll find a nice boy for you to marry. That's what her aunt had promised, but from the very first day she arrived in Songjeong-ri after leaving her grandfather in Jigyeong-ri, Sunil gave up all hope of her aunt fulfilling her promise. Her aunt had seven children. She and her husband were liquor wholesalers at the market, and were busy shuttling between factories, retailers, and other markets all day, leaving them with no time to look after the kids. All the laundry, cooking, and cleaning up after dinner ensured there was always a mountain of work ahead of Sunil. Her aunt's house was a dirt-floor shanty not far from the cattle yard where an auction took place every week, built with cargo junk from the U.S. Army, pieces of slate, and scraps salvaged from wooden crates and cardboard boxes covered with tar. From the very first evening Sunil arrived, she took on all the housework for ten people, including her aunt, uncle, and herself.

Nice things.

That's what her aunt had promised Sunil, but in that house, nice things could never come to her. If she grilled meat or fish, her aunt watched her like a hawk, and only her uncle, the eldest daughter, who was the firstborn, or the eldest son, who was the fourth oldest, were allowed to bring the dish to the table. Sunil went to bed at one in the morning and got up at six. She got by on leftovers that were never enough, and though she was overworked, she tried her best to look clean and presentable. She never went outside with disheveled hair, and if she wore a blouse, she made sure it was buttoned all the way up to her neck. When she walked through the market, holding the hands of her young cousins whom she'd cleaned up and neatly dressed, the merchants would come out and watch them go by. You don't know how many maids threw up their hands and ran away from that house, but look at that girl, look what she's pulled off.

Sunil's aunt and uncle monitored her outings, at first saying it was too dangerous for a young girl to be out alone, and later arguing that it was equally dangerous for a young woman. The neighborhood isn't safe. You have no idea what can happen to a nice girl like you. And it's not like you can go to school, since you don't even know the basics. Since they didn't send her to school, Sunil had to stay home. She did the laundry and the cooking, made banchan, and looked after her cousins. There was never enough water for ten people. With no other water facilities in the area, a public well located about a hundred meters southwest of the cattle yard was the main source for many families, but it was so frequently used that there was hardly any chance for it to refill. If Sunil was busy with house-work and arrived late, she would find the water level reduced to mere dirt. After several failed attempts to fetch water, Sunil started going to the well at three in the morning. When she set her empty container by the well and peered down over the edge, water like black oil lapped below. Since the well didn't have a pulley, she would manually lower the bucket, fill it, lift it up, and dump the water into her own container, repeating this process until her container was full. After lugging the container back to the house five times, her arms would be numb and her clothes wet, and she would be so sleepy that she could hardly continue. If her two oldest cousins, who did attend school, washed their hair in the morning, Sunil would run out of water to do the dinner dishes.

When Sunil had been living there for about a year, her aunt and uncle hired workers to dig a well in their kitchen. They dug for days, heaping red soil that smelled like manure on the kitchen floor, and in the end, succeeded in creating a well one hundred twenty meters deep. The workers covered the outside wall with cement, raising the opening about waist high, and attached a pulley. They also spread cement on the ground by the well so that laundry and food preparation could be done there. It was nice, but now that they had their own well, Sunil could no longer leave the house. There was no reason for her to, unless she had to go to the market to buy groceries or deliver lunch to her aunt and uncle. Her days were busy, but they passed quietly. At the water-stained well, which smelled like dish soap and green onion roots, time evaporated like water in a shallow dish, left out in the sun. **No one is coming**. As she salted a crate of croakers, she thought, No one knows I'm here. **That's why no one is coming**.

Sunja.

One day her aunt came into the kitchen and said their neighbor was going to draw water from their well starting tomorrow. They would pay fifty won per month to use their well, even though it cost twenty won for just two buckets of water delivered from the market. Her aunt didn't seem too happy about that.

The next day, the neighbor girl came to draw water. She had broad, hunched shoulders, narrow eyes in an angular face, and tightly pursed lips as if she had something in her mouth, giving the impression of a smile. Sunil knew the girl's name was also Sunja and that she attended an all-girls' school. She knew Sunja had an older brother who often didn't come home and a mother with a drinking habit who earned a living by grinding red pepper, green pepper, and garlic in a tiny stall at the market. Sunil knew these things just from what she heard through the plywood walls separating the shanties, which were less than an inch thick and insufficient to block out noise from next door. Sunja entered the kitchen without a greeting, drew water in silence, and then left. She wore socks with her school dress shoes. Seeing the stretched-out socks Sunja had pulled up her calves, Sunil realized the girl also knew. She knows my name is Sunja too.

Sunja.

Hey, Sunja.

Because that's what everyone called me.

•

Sunja lived next door she was my friend

She went to a girls high school in Yeongdeungpo but somehow we got to know each other we were close

If I went to her house because I wanted a little break

my uncle would come after me and ask why I kept going over there did they feed me or give me things he would cause such a scene

so her ma said don't come around here anymore

I never got enough food enough sleep enough clothes

I can't take it anymore I need to get out of here do you know a place I could go

The day Sunja got paid we ate black bean noodles together it was the best thing to eat back then

I asked her can you find a place for me I can't live like this anymore

She knew everything how I had to work all the time

Everyone wanted to make me their daughter-in-law the neighbors the market merchants even young men

I was neat and young with long hair

always nicely combed braided or tied back and always home just working

The only times I'd come out was to buy something at the market and when I did

they said they wanted to marry me or they had a nice man for me

My aunt said no because I was too young then they said how about let them get engaged

and they can marry later

They always said that

It's because I was a good girl and all I did was work so they wanted to make me their daughter-in-law

Come on run away

That Sunja put you up to it didn't she

I'll find a job for you just say you're going to your grandfather's in Gangwon Province

Come on let's run away

Sunja found a job for me at a clinic they are looking for a nurse's aide it's around Namdaemun

She wrote down the address

When I told my aunt I wanted to go back to Gangwon Province she asked me why when she was going to send me to school

Only then she said that so I wouldn't go

Mom, my friend's mom died recently, Sejin said. I went to the funeral and found out her mom's name was Sunja. And there's this homestyle restaurant near the studio that I go to sometimes. It's been there for thirty-five years, and I recently learned the owner's name is also Sunja. Cho Sunja. Another Sunja.

Yup.

Is it *Sun* (順) for *gentle* and *ja* (者) for *person*?

Out of breath, Sunil realized she was walking too fast, and slowed down. *Sun* (順) for *gentle* and *ja* (子) for *child*. Junko, gentle child. I'd thought that was my name. That's why I was Sunja. And my friend was Sunja, too. Sunja was Sunja's friend.

Back then, I'd done everything with Sunja, Sunil thought, her face turning red from holding in a cough. Everything with Sunja. It was Sunja who'd urged her to go to the clinic, saying it was strange her cough had lingered for three months. It was Sunja who had gone with her, and after she was diagnosed with tuberculosis and had to stay in the corner room, it was Sunja who brought her some freshly grilled croaker or a warm rice ball with beans. It was Sunja who taught her how to knit sweaters and mittens using blue wool, it was Sunja she went with to the theater to watch a movie. Sometimes when my mom is beating me, I think about you on the other side of the wall, Sunja had said. Go ahead and hit me just kill me why don't you if I scream Sunja will hear Sunja is listening Sunja is listening right now. Then even if I feel like I'm going to die that second, I won't be scared anymore I'd suddenly feel brave. This is what Sunja had said.

Sunja said she wanted to be a teacher. And after she became a teacher, she wanted to study more and become a vice-principal or principal. Sunil believed Sunja would. Because Sunja works hard, Sunil thought, awestruck. Not only is she good at making everything, but she has really great penmanship. Whenever Sunja would take notes in her small notebook or spread open her Union English textbook and copy out the English phrases, Sunil would push the basket of knitting aside and stare at Sunja's writing. They were only letters, but they were like Sunja. Like her mind, poised, strong, with a quirky sense of humor. Sunil kept Sunja's old notebook in her room and learned how to write by copying out Sunja's writing.

Oh my, you have such nice writing.

When Yeongjin's fifth grade teacher praised Sunil's penmanship, Sunil was stunned and thought about Sunja for the first time in decades.

Was Sunja alive? Was she still alive somewhere?

Sunil realized she'd reached an age where she not only wondered how Sunja was doing but also whether she was still alive.

I need to run away.

In 1976, Sunil got on a city bus. She snuck out of the house, walked to a bus stop far from the market, and then to the next one, finally catching a bus that was running late. Sitting against a window coated with dirt from the dusty roads, she looked out the opposite window as the bus rattled through Yeongdeungpo and crossed the Second Han River Bridge. Gazing out at the Han River, so vast she'd once mistook it for the sea when she first came to Gwangnaru with Grandfather, she found it strange that she didn't have many memories of being a refugee. That's right, Grandfather smacked me in the head, because I was so sleepy I almost passed out while walking. After Sunil crossed the bridge, she reached City Hall and continued on to Namdaemun. Asking for directions multiple times with just an address in hand, she finally arrived at a previously Japanese-owned wooden house that had been converted into a private clinic. In the garden were black stones, peonies, and golden marigolds. The doctor's wife—whose contact Sunja had obtained for Sunil through the sister of a friend of a classmate at school—was the only nurse at the clinic. She didn't handle other matters, except for administering shots to patients. Wearing her hair twisted up like the actress Um Aing-ran from *Barefooted Youth* and a sleeveless dress with a cropped cardigan covering her shoulders, she stayed either in the garden or at the private residence at the back of the clinic. She taught Sunil how to administer shots. How to rub a cotton ball or piece of cloth moistened with alcohol on the skin, insert the needle, tie a band around the arm to find a vein, and prick with a needle. She also showed her how to differentiate between the little glass vials on the medicine shelf, identifying which were antibiotics and which were anti-inflammatories. When the doctor, who was also the director of the clinic, sent a patient out of his office with instructions like "1 cc or 2 cc of mycin," Sunil would carefully draw the medicine into the syringe to the prescribed dosage and administer the shot. There weren't many beds, but there were quite a few inpatients, and incinerating their bedside waste, washing the linens, disinfecting the medical equipment, and mopping the floor were all part of Sunil's job. There was a lot of work and the pay was very little because she was provided room and board, but it was much better than being at her aunt's house. She could also sit in on the English class that the doctor's wife took once a week. Most of the time, Sunil had no idea what the English teacher and doctor's wife were saying, since the class had been ongoing for several months, but she sat and listened regardless, trying to memorize what she heard.

The doctor asked Sunil if she knew that Korean nurses were being recruited to work in Germany. I know a Catholic priest who helps send people there. If you study English and work hard at your job, I'll introduce you to him.

Germany.

Where on earth was that?

About three or four months ago, Sunil had glimpsed Germany through the photos Sejin showed her after returning from her trip. The angels of Berlin with golden, outspread wings and weapons in their hands; the bullet-scarred Victory Column; the wheat fields of Bochum and people on yachts on the Ruhr River; the black spires and iron bridge of Cologne; the vaulted ceiling of the Frankfurt Central Station; the red roofs and attic windows of Munich. Listening to Sejin describe this place and that, and all she had seen, Sunil thought about how different they were from what she had imagined. Germany. What kind of place was Germany? A place where both the educated and uneducated could start over, a place that didn't ask or care if you got married or not, or if you were a virgin or not, a place far, far away, reached by going higher than the clouds and faster than the wind, a place that surged like a cliff and then sank like mud in Sunil's dreams.

About half a year into her stay at the clinic, Sunil was carrying a bucket of lye into the yard when she found her uncle standing there. He seized her on the spot and dragged her back to their house. Her aunt beat the terrified Sunil, whose face had drained of all color, punching her in the back and shoulders, and went on about her grandfather's health. Because of you, your grandfather. Because you ran away, your poor grandfather. Worried sick, that old man. Sunil ate nothing and sat in the corner of the room, mentally tearing her aunt and uncle and grandfather to pieces, over and over again, then finally wondered: Who told them I was there? Who knew I was there?

Two weeks went by before she saw Sunja again. She came in while Sunil was sitting by the well, peeling a potato that had been soaking in water. Sunja said she wasn't allowed to fetch water from this well anymore. Actually, it was Auntie who'd said that. How had she put it? That girl can't come here anymore. That bitch can't come see you anymore, she'd said. Sunja just stood there. She didn't ask me what I was doing back or what had happened, she didn't even say she was sorry. She just stood there, not saying anything to me. I didn't want to look at her anymore and wished she would just leave, but she continued to stand there. Not knowing what else to do, I slapped her, wishing she would just go away. I slapped her in the face. But she didn't cry.

•

Fires often broke out back then. It was because many homes still used oil lamps at night, and houses were stuck next to each other, their walls made of oiled strawboard and wood, and roofs made of fabric. Shacks would turn to ashes overnight and people would die, all because a lamp got knocked over. If tarps or canvases caught fire, the flame spread quickly, leaving no chance for anyone to douse it with a bucket of water. At the sound of someone shouting "Fire!" the whole neighborhood would jump out of their beds like magic and run outside. The same happened that night.

Fire!

No one died or was seriously injured, but a few shanties went up in flames. Her aunt's home was one of them. After sitting in the cattle yard with the other residents who had evacuated, waiting for the sun to rise, Sunil went back to her aunt's house to find there was nothing left except the well, surrounded by rubble. She saw Sunja lift an ash-covered board and fish out something that looked like a sweater. Next to her, Sunja's mother was struggling to scrape off a bit of gold that was stuck to the scorched remains of a drawer. Most of the people who had lost their homes and possessions were market merchants, who generally managed to carry on with their businesses, but Sunja's mother wasn't able to do the same. She sat at her market stall, looking exhausted and ill, and then one day the mother and daughter disappeared without any explanation.

Sunil's aunt and uncle set up a tent where their house had once stood, living there for some time until they made plans to leave for Busan, where her uncle's family had a business. The last thing Sunil wanted was to continue living with this family, and so she resolved to get married. She met Han Jungeon through a merchant at the market and decided on a whim that he would do. Like her, Jungeon had been orphaned during the war, and had no family or money to his name, but he was literate, even knowing some Chinese characters, smiled easily, and worked hard. Sunil believed that was enough. As long as you worked hard, it was enough. Her aunt and uncle were against her marrying, but Sunil was in her twenties now, so they had no good reason to oppose the marriage. They vowed they wouldn't attend the wedding, since she insisted on going through with a union they were clearly against, but in the end, they invited their own guests to the ceremony, collected the cash gifts, and took off. Sunil stayed on at the market. Her aunt contacted her once in a while, but there was very little communication between them. Her aunt died many years ago. Sunil heard their second or third daughter's marriage had been a mess and her aunt had been traveling far from home, trying to fix it, when she got food poisoning and suddenly died. And it was only long after she had died that Sunil received the news.

In the process of verifying her place of family origin to enter herself in Jungeon's family register, Sunil learned that her birth name was recorded in the original register as Yi Sunil and that her little sister, born in 1948, was recorded as Eunil. Yi Eunil. According to the records, her sister wasn't marked as deceased. She was still alive. So were her parents. Her father, mother, and sister—all alive still. Names unknown to others remained on that piece of paper, forgotten like a small, neglected plot of land deep in the woods. After crossing out her own name to register her marriage, as well as the names of her family to register their deaths, Sunil wiped the document from her memory. She forgot about the Xs marked neatly over the names and the Chinese character 亡 for *deceased* that was recorded there. When Sunil's life comes to an end, those forgotten names will cease to exist for good. She had no intention of passing on the things those names had experienced. She'd never told anyone. She knew it was possible to leave something behind in speech or writing, that there were those who had succeeded in doing exactly that, but it wasn't what she wanted. All those horrific stories . . . Do I have to keep thinking about them and talking about them? Sunil hoped her children, Yeongjin, Sejin and Mansu, would never have to experience those things, even as stories.

Sunil's grandfather died in the late 1970s. By the time she received the call, the village elders had already buried him on the mountain. She was enraged when she heard the news. She believed what she felt was rage. What else could it be?

How could he die? she thought. So the old man means to torture me until the end?

Even so, she set a bowl of cooked rice and a bowl of water on the wood stove for half a day so that he could eat and drink before going on his way. Though she rarely thought of him, she'd never forgotten the money he'd brought to her wedding in one of those yellow medication envelopes, and she found herself thinking of it from time to time. I'd kept that envelope in my hanbok sleeve and then I'd lost it. I know you must have had a hard life, too, Grandfather, so rest now, rest in peace wherever you are, she prayed. It was after the mid-1980s that she started tending his grave. Then in 1986 . . . When the whole country was abuzz with the

Asian Games being held in Seoul, she received an international call. A woman with a high, raspy voice called her by her childhood name.

Sunja, is that you?

Pardon?

Sunja.

Who's this?

Aren't you Sunja, the daughter of Yun Okyeong who used to live in Cheorwon?

Who's this? Who are you? Sunil demanded, feeling rage and terror at the caller who kept calling her by her childhood name without revealing her identity. The woman said she was her aunt.

It's me, Bukyeong, your ma's sister. Okyeong eonni's little sis.

Fed up with being poor and uneducated, Bukyeong had left home shortly after Korea's liberation from Japan. She lived in Seoul under the U.S. military government, evacuated to Geoje Island when the Korean War broke out, and then married an American soldier she'd met there. After the war, she went to America with him. Since she was from Daek-magoji, which had been close to all the fighting, she'd assumed everyone back home had died. Plus, she couldn't speak a word of English, so she'd had a hard time adjusting to her husband's country, and had lived in the same place until now, just getting by. Her kids were grown now, and she'd been thinking more and more of home lately, when she happened to run into someone from her hometown, who told her there was one left.

There's one left.

The only one alive.

That aunt was now dead, too. Her liver disease got worse, and she passed away in April of 2003. During the seventeen years from when she first got in touch with Sunil until she passed away, she visited Korea five times. Meanwhile, her American husband died of a stroke while out fishing alone on a lake, and her son ended up having a daughter. Auntie's son, he accompanied her every time she came to Korea, but he was more like his father than his mother. He was a soldier like his father, and couldn't speak Korean. He was the one who had called Sunil to let her know of his mother's death.

Sunja? Umma's dead, he said in Korean.

Dead?

Dead.

•

When Sunil had gone to Deoksugung Palace to meet Bukyeong the first time she came back to Korea, Sunil had worn a hanbok. She thought she should wear her best, and it had been her best. It was 1987 and the day was clear, but the smell of tear gas lingered in the air. She'd planned to go to City Hall Station, but took the wrong bus, and ended up getting off at Gwanghwamun instead. She walked past the Koreana Hotel to Deoksugung Palace. There was no shade, so it was difficult to keep her eyes open. Neither could she walk quickly, because the hem of her hanbok skirt kept getting tangled around her ankles, and her face and back were sticky with sweat. Would she be able to recognize her aunt? How was she supposed to find someone she had never seen before in a crowd? Sunil worried as she walked along the palace stone wall, but her aunt came squinting from the opposite direction. They resembled each other so much that there was no need to ask. So Sunja . . .

it was only then that I realized I looked like my mother

Mom.

What are you thinking about?

Everything okay? Sejin asked.

Sunil looked up from the hiking boots. Sejin was staring at Sunil with eyes that were slightly puffy. Her hastily tied hair showed signs of gray.

She's got her father's wispy eyebrows and my round eyes and forehead. This child had also grown up in the market. The merchants used to call her Bashful, because she'd clamp her lips together and stare at the ground, though she talked easily enough with her siblings. Sunil hoped Sejin would have a nice life. But this one didn't know the first thing about housework. She left a stainless-steel steamer on the stove until all the water in the pot had boiled away, and she poured boiling water into a regular glass cup without first placing a metal spoon in it. Many times she'd be holding a glass bottle or cup and it would slip from her hands. But the other kids were no different. Kids with a weak grip. Kids who couldn't take hold of something, who'd get swept away and vanish if something ever happened to them.

A nice life.

But what was a nice life, Sunil wondered.

I'd wished that for my kids. I'd wished they would grow into adults without experiencing anything terrible, that they'd be happy. I'd wished for these things without knowing anything. I didn't know anything.

Do you need them, too?

Sejin blinked at Sunil's question as if she didn't understand.

Huh? You mean hiking boots?

Yeah, like these.

No, I don't hike.

You don't?

Nope.

I'm sure you'll have a chance to use them. Let's buy a pair for you, too.

No, no, I don't need them.

No?

Really, I don't need them.

You sure?

Sunil turned to look at the boots again, but her eyes and nose suddenly burned, and she had to take a deep breath. I need them, Yeongjin had said last Thursday, digging through the shoe cabinet. Mom, have you seen my hiking boots? But even after rummaging through the shoe cabinets in both apartments, as well as through several boxes, she hadn't been able to find them. Where did they go? My boots, Yeongjin muttered. She and her coworkers from the store were going hiking on the weekend. Mom, I can't find my boots. Sunil believed the boots were there somewhere and told her so, leaving Yeongjin to keep looking. But no matter how much Yeongjin looked, they were nowhere to be seen. Then Sunil remembered wearing the hiking boots in Jigyeong-ri a few years back, the ones that had fallen apart in a rice paddy. The soles had come off in the mud. Sunil grew so angry that she whipped around, holding the ladle she'd been stirring the pot with in one hand, and shouted at Yeongjin. Why are you looking for them now? You left them to rot, unused, in the box, and now you're looking for them like a fool?

Yeongjin had asked her why. Why did you take them without asking me? Why did you leave them there? They were mine.

You didn't even ask me, you just took them and ruined them and left them there.

Why did you leave them in the paddy?

Realizing they weren't actually questions, Sunil closed her mouth.

What was Yeongjin's shoe size? Sometimes a 235-mm shoe size was a bit too small or too big. Because Yeongjin didn't drink enough water and was on her feet all day, breathing in dust, her feet often swelled, causing her shoe size to change frequently. Sunil clenched and unclenched her left hand, gazing down at the hiking boots on the floor. Her thumb still prickled from the night before. She'd been draining hot water after boiling some fiddleheads and had spilled some on her thumb. The water had been scalding, but she hadn't moved, tilting the heavy pot at an angle to avoid spilling the fiddleheads down the drain. Her hand still prickled and stung.

The fact that her hands, weathered and hardened from decades of cooking and cleaning, still found some things unbearably hot both upset and amazed her. Sunil remembered the woman who sold soondae at the market in Gonghang-dong, how red and ripe her hands had seemed. When Sunil asked for some soondae, the woman grasped a knife in her right hand and stuck her left hand in the scorching steamer to pick out the cooked sausage and slice it up. While she sliced it into bite-size pieces on the chopping board, she pressed down on the sausage with her left hand, curled as if she were holding an egg. She jerked away her hand as if she'd burned herself, only to bring it back down on the soondae. Ma'am, do they still feel hot to you, even when you've touched them all your life? But of course, Sunil would never ask her such a thing, so she had simply stood there, saying only that she needed just a little seasoning.

Sunil picked up the boots and asked if he had something else, something better. Whether today or tomorrow, Sunil hoped she'd find a good pair of hiking boots. In the evening when Yeongjin came home from work, Sunil would urge her to try on the new boots. She'd tell her to try them on, that she'd exchange them if they didn't fit. Sunil might even say she was sorry. After all, what was so hard about that, what was so hard about saying sorry?

•

But Sunil knew there were things Yeongjin would never say.

She believed it was because Yeongjin could never forgive her. And that's why I won't bring up what that child won't say.

Sunil knew that some things in life could never be forgiven.

Because even Sunja had things she couldn't forgive.

things to come

I shall drink dirty water from ditches and die there.

Han Sejin remembers the night Ha Miyeong said these words. Summer, the evening breeze was cool, and they had opened the big window and sat by it, looking outside. The moths had been hovering, hitting their wings against the streetlamp, and the smell of laundry wafted up from the downstairs apartment. I shall drink water from ditches and die there. Miyeong said it was from a Virginia Woolf book, maybe those weren't the exact words, but they were close, and after she'd read that line, she'd thought about it often. And if she kept thinking about it, she'd arrive at the conclusion that, ultimately, she would not be able to escape from here. She had believed she'd be able to do a lot more when she became an adult.

Miyeong said maybe becoming an adult was the same as eating food that fell on the ground. Choosing the least dirty piece from what was already contaminated, brushing off the dirt, and then eating what still seemed edible, maybe that's what it meant to be an adult. Was it like forgetting? My father said forgetting was the secret to life. But I had a strange memory, a memory of my mother throwing a baby. We were sitting on the floor with our backs against the wall and my mother was trying to console the baby in her arms when she suddenly threw it. With a thump, the baby fell onto the blanket spread on the floor. I saw it. It was such a strange memory that I assumed it must have been a dream or my imagination, but when I mentioned it to my father a few years ago, he let out a big sigh. That baby wasn't the only thing she threw. She did that to you and your younger sister and . . . I realized then that my mother was someone who had been doing these things for a long time, and my father, knowing all this, still left us with her. Whenever I got upset because of my parents, he told me to forget, that I needed to forget if I wanted peace. He said that was the secret to life. When I first heard him say that, I was so angry I was stunned, but these days I keep thinking about what he said. Just forget. If you can't forgive, forget. But what if that really was the secret? Miyeong had remained silent for a long time after, finally saying it was difficult to think clearly about these things.

Some time after that summer evening, Miyeong backed away from the living room coffee table and stepped on the cat with her slippered foot.

Around that time, Miyeong often quit in the middle of things. She would put down a book or stop a movie halfway through. Midway through Rebecca Solnit's *Wanderlust*, she quit, saying she found the writing too dense, and while watching Mia Hansen-Løve's *Things to Come* (*L'Avenir*), she turned it off, saying it was too fast-paced. Still, Miyeong managed to finish it. She said all the scenes from the movie read as words on a page, as something that should be consumed slowly, like a book, because sentences that should have spanned dozens of pages rushed by on-screen at a breakneck pace in just a few seconds. Why is Nathalie so busy? How can she carry on without collapsing when she's so busy? Since she needed to take breaks, Miyeong took two and a half hours to watch the whole movie, which had a running time of about a hundred minutes. After this experience, she watched fewer movies. It seemed she couldn't muster the nerve. On Friday or Saturday evenings, she would browse the titles that showed up on their streaming platform, searching for what seemed to Sejin, movies that wouldn't feel like reading words on a page. However, there weren't many movies that met this description, so Miyeong gradually watched fewer and fewer movies.

One weekend, after Sejin and Miyeong finished washing and drying the laundry earlier than usual, they agreed to watch a movie while eating some snacks. They chose an action flick featuring a reserved main character with a painful past, a colleague who worries about him yet assigns him to a dangerous mission, with a hostage that the main character must rescue. After venturing into the gang's hideout to rescue the hostage, the central character strangles the gang members and blasts holes through their chests, and just when he is about to stab the boss's face with the end of a farm tool, Sejin heard Miyeong whisper to her to stop the movie. Miyeong was panting, her face drained of color, her skin clammy with sweat. She said she felt as though her blood had stopped and there wasn't enough oxygen in the room. She had difficulty breathing, so Sejin found a clean plastic bag in the kitchen and held it to Miyeong's mouth. Miyeong breathed in and out, clutching the bag, her breath beading inside the plastic. When she exhaled, the bag swelled, and when she inhaled, the bag shriveled up to her mouth. She said she couldn't take someone getting hurt, even if it wasn't real.

It looked so real, as if someone was dying in front of my eyes, and I couldn't keep watching.

After Miyeong stepped on the cat, she fell.

In her effort to avoid stepping on it, she'd ended up stepping on it many times, and in her effort not to fall, she'd ended up having an especially bad fall. Sejin had been wiping dried soap scum off the mirror with a finger while brushing her teeth when she'd heard several shrieks and then a thud that shook the floor. She ran into the living room and found Miyeong on the floor. She had fallen backward, but was twisted at the waist, lying prone with her palms planted on the floor. The cat, the cat, Miyeong screamed. She asked Sejin if the cat was okay. While Sejin examined the cat, Miyeong lay where she was. After Sejin helped her to the bed, Miyeong continued to sweat and weep. Miyeong said she'd stepped on the cat's paws multiple times. It was trying to run away, but I kept stepping on those tiny paws. And then I squashed it under my back. It was horrible.

Stop it.

Sejin reassured Miyeong the cat was fine and that the moment had passed, but after that night, Miyeong found a hospital, packed a few of her things, and checked herself in. On the front lawn of the hospital stood a large dawn redwood as tall as the fourth floor. Sejin and Miyeong sat at a wobbly round table in the reception area, waiting for Miyeong to be assigned a room and bed. A staff member appeared and called Miyeong's name. Her books and clothes were packed in a paper shopping bag with a rope handle. He asked to examine the bag and peered inside. With thin, blunt fingers, he carefully untied the rope, which he handed to Sejin, and then returned the bag minus the handle to Miyeong. Miyeong hugged the bag to her chest and got into the elevator that would take her to her room. Sejin was not allowed to go any further. See you, Miyeong said. I'll come pick you up, Sejin said.

Sejin drove home. She opened the fridge to get some water and saw an apple from which Miyeong had taken a few bites. The inside was a bit dry, but hadn't yet browned. The bite marks were distinct.

Stop it.

Sejin regretted saying those words to Miyeong. She sat, turning the apple over a little in her hand, and then cut off the dry parts and ate the rest. The cat came and wrapped its tail around her leg. Sejin remembered she needed to find a cat-sitter for her upcoming trip to New York. She decided to come home ten days earlier.

•

Park Munil, who had come through JFK airport three or four years ago, warned Sejin she might be subjected to some unpleasant measures at airport security, but she experienced nothing of the sort. She believed the late hour had something to do with it. It was close to midnight. The quarantine officers and security guards merely looked tired and sleepy. Near the baggage claim, an airport agent with a scarf around her neck shouted at people to move forward and keep the exit clear. Practically thrust across the small lobby by the agent, Sejin stepped outside the building and confronted chaos. It was cold and raining, with shouts exchanged between cabbies and Uber drivers picking up passengers, profanities yelled at people dragging their luggage into the middle of the street to climb into their rides, profanities hurled at profanities . . . Sejin stood under the awning, listening to all the *shits* and *fucks* coming from every direction, until the Uber she and her party had requested arrived.

The driver, in a Ford with paint peeling off the door handle, was wearing a wrinkled T-shirt and shorts. With a bent index finger, he counted the people in their group—one, two, three—and said, Okay. He wasn't talkative, but seemed to have a habit of talking to himself. He hauled an oversized stuffed rabbit with long ears from the backseat, jammed it into the trunk, and gestured for them to put their luggage in the trunk as well. Sejin and her party climbed into the backseat, where an empty foam cup with a straw was rolling around on the floor, and headed for their hotel in Brooklyn. Located a little south of Walt Whitman Park, their hotel was a tall, nondescript building on a street no different from any main road in Seoul. Sejin walked through the lobby, which smelled of cinnamon, sugar, and vanilla, and went up to her room. She took off her shoes at the entrance by the mirror, walked across the carpet in her socked feet, and sat at the foot of the bed. The odor of furniture cleaner hung in the air, and only then did she feel that she had arrived in a new place. A picture frame hung on the opposite wall. She gazed at the bold white letters against a black background and realized they were the names of nearby places. CONEY ISLAND, DUMBO, BROOKLYN HEIGHTS, STATEN ISLAND, FLATBUSH AVE., ROCKAWAY BEACH . . .

Would Miyeong be able to come to the phone? Sejin calculated the time difference and called the hospital, asking if she could speak to Miyeong. Sejin was swallowing to pop her left ear, still clogged after the flight, when Miyeong came on the line.

You just arrived?

Yup.

Are you at the hotel?

Yup.

How is it?

The bed's big. I don't like the way it smells. It's raining.

Miyeong asked how things had been at the airport. Sejin said she'd heard people say *shit* and *fuck*, but it had sounded exactly like the Korean words for *shit* and *fuck*, and just like how Koreans start by shouting, Yea, yea, when they're angry at someone, everyone here was shouting, Yea, yea, in English. But the feel of those words was exactly the same as in Korean, so it was strange and funny. Miyeong laughed and said all the countries in the world probably shared the nuance of hatred. That's probably why swear words are so easy and powerful. Yeah, probably. Miyeong said she'd had soybean sprout soup for lunch and that she was about to go for a stroll in the garden. They have so many four o'clock flowers in the garden.

Really?

So you're going to bed?

Yeah. It's past midnight here.

Okay, goodnight then.

Have a nice walk.

After Sejin hung up, she remained sitting on the bed. The pressure imbalance in her ears made her left cheek tingle, as if she'd been slapped. She moved her jaw to the left and right, and stared at the place names in the frame. Coney, Dumbo, Brooklyn, Staten, Flatbush . . . Sejin couldn't remember when she'd first seen the lights of this city. She thought she'd seen them for the first time when the plane was flying over, preparing to land at JFK, but maybe she hadn't. After all, this city's nightscape was already familiar to her through various forms of media. When she said she would be participating in a book festival in New York for five days, Norman said he'd come. Really? Isn't it far from where you live? It was about 250 miles from Virginia to New York, Norman said, but if he drove through Baltimore, it would take him a little over four hours by car.

Sejin was in high school the last time she saw Norman Kylie. The year was 1996 and Norman was a soldier, and it was the year his daughter, Jamie, turned one. As the son of Yun Bukyeong, the sister of Sejin's grandmother, Norman accompanied Bukyeong on each of her visits to Korea, but 1996 turned out to be their last. Afterward, Bukyeong's health declined rapidly, and she could no longer handle long-distance flights. In 1999 and 2001, she called Sunil in the middle of the night, weeping, saying Korea was too far away and that she no longer had the energy to travel such a distance. She passed away in Virginia. Following her death, Norman occasionally called Sejin. Their phone calls were usually brief. Sejin wasn't fluent in English, and Norman couldn't speak Korean, so they mostly exchanged conventional greetings.

How are you?

I'm good. How is Jamie?

Jamie's good, too.

Everyone's well?

Everyone's well.

Hope to see you soon.

Norman sometimes asked after Sunil.

Your mom and my mom sure looked alike, didn't they. They sure did. Not like aunt and niece, but more like sisters . . . Like a mirror image of the past and present . . .

Norman and Sejin had been present at the first meeting between Bukyeong and Sunil in Korea. Sejin had accompanied Sunil, and Norman had accompanied Bukyeong.

As the two women wept, touching each other's shoulders and faces by the stonewall of Deoksugung Palace, Norman and Sejin gazed awkwardly at each other. Norman hunched his shoulders in embarrassment, tears brimming in his eyes. Sejin was frightened to see her mother wail loudly in the middle of the street. She was frightened by this stranger who had appeared out of nowhere, wearing her mother's face, and by Norman, who was dressed in his military uniform. Norman looked frightened, too, which further frightened Sejin. After all, Norman was an adult, and she was only nine, and he appeared to be on the brink of tears.

Witnesses.

It was only after some time had passed that she thought of herself and Norman as such.

When Norman's daughter, Jamie, was ten years old, her facial nerves were damaged in a serious car accident. It seemed Norman's family was on the verge of bankruptcy due to Jamie's medical bills and multiple surgeries. When Sejin was in university, Norman called once to ask if he could borrow money. Though he didn't go into detail, he mentioned that he and his wife were living out of their car. Sejin managed to scrounge up five hundred dollars and wired it to the account Norman provided. After that, she thought about Norman and the money. What could he possibly do with such an amount? She thought about the level of destitution that would lead someone to call a relative in Korea for money, the destitution that Norman and his family were experiencing in America.

You'll have to drive for four hours?

Sejin said it was too far. Norman hesitated as if he hadn't expected her to respond that way and said listlessly that four hours wasn't too bad. In America, that's not very far. Okay, then come. All right, I will. Anyway, is everyone well? Everyone's well. See you soon. Take care. Take care. After she hung up, she realized she hadn't told Norman the exact dates she would be in New York. She wondered if she should call him back, but she didn't. And neither did Norman call Sejin to ask.

•

Sejin woke to the sound of someone coughing in the next room. The sun hadn't come up yet and it was too early to go down for breakfast. She threw on a light windbreaker and stepped out onto the early morning street. After crossing a few intersections, she was heading north along a small park on her right when her eyes registered a familiar word on a metal plate fixed to an iron railing. She stopped. KOREAN WAR . . . VET-ERANS PLAZA. What looked like a sugar maple leaf was engraved beneath the letters, as if it were the park's symbol. Sejin stepped into the narrow space, which hardly felt like a plaza, and thought the leaf engraved on the plate might actually be from a silver maple or sycamore, not a sugar maple. Sycamore trees, their bases covered in moss, lined the path, leaning toward the East River. The grass and concrete slabs were wet with dew and morning fog. After cutting through the park and reaching the north entrance, Sejin saw a simple monument of rectangular granite blocks that had been joined and stacked together. She read the inscribed names, the smell of garbage wafting up from the sidewalk. June 26, 1950 to July 27, 1953. Korean War Veteran Chapter #171. Brooklyn, NY.

She walked west toward the river and found herself under the Brooklyn Bridge. Tilting her head back, she stared up at the steel cables resembling the thigh bones of a gigantic beast, holding up the roadway in the air. Should I go up to the bridge? If she did, she'd have to go across the river and then make her way back again. The thought so drained her that she started walking along the river instead. The day was slowly dawning. It was early, but there were people on the river-bank. Maybe they had spent the night there. She stood next to an old man sitting on one of the wide steps that led down to the river, eating something wrapped in butcher paper. She looked across the East River at Manhattan—a borough she felt she knew, because of all that she'd seen and heard, despite never having set foot in it—and saw two beams of light reaching up into the darkness from between buildings. Sejin sat by the river for about an hour, and as the glass façades of Manhattan skyscrapers turned orange from the early morning rays, she stood up. She took a different route back to the hotel.

Sejin went up to her room and then came back down to the dining area for breakfast. As soon as the elevator doors opened on the ground floor, the smell of flour, egg, cinnamon, and sugar hit her. In the dining area, hotel guests were making waffles. The waffle mixture was grayish, like papier-mâché. People tipped the plastic jug, pouring the mixture into the hot iron, and waited for the timer to go off. When the timer signaled that their waffles were done, they transferred the browned waffles onto Styrofoam plates and left. Sejin realized the sweet scent that filled the hotel lobby, that lingered in the rooms, and even on her hair, despite just having shampooed it, came from the cooking of the waffle mixture. She avoided the iron, and instead put some grapes and pieces of cantaloupe and grapefruit on her plate, and poured coffee into a large mug. She sat with her back to the window overlooking the street, just as the rest of her group—Park Munil, Moon Haeri, and Lee Junguen— came down to the dining area, their faces puffy from the long flight. They joined her at her table.

They were scheduled to have a conversation with two American writers in Queens that day: an openly gay novelist of Korean descent and an essayist who was also a poet, playwright, and radio DJ. The title of their talk was "Reading Peace, Writing Resistance." The organizers seemed to hope that these Korean writers, coming from a divided country still technically at war since only an armistice was declared, would discuss peace and perhaps comment on the 2016 Candlelight Protests in Korea.

Haeri mentioned the talk might be challenging to manage due to the overly broad subject and lack of specific questions. Munil said it was unclear who would serve as the moderator, and Jungeun declared that regardless of the subject, he planned to talk about the globalization of American capitalism and its harmful impact on both the Korean labor market and the environment. I mean, just look at that. He pointed at the two oversized garbage bins near the dining area entrance. Look at what they're doing. The bins, about 1 x 1.5 meters in size and lacking lids, presumably for convenience, had a piece of paper labeled RECYCLE on the right one. However, guests ignored this, tossing used paper napkins and dirty plates with leftover food into both bins.

They took an Uber to Queens. Because of all the traffic, they got out of the car about one hundred meters from their destination and walked the rest of the way. However, there were so many pedestrians that traveling on foot wasn't easy. They crossed the street in front of a supermarket that had an outdoor display of piles of donut peaches, wizened by the heat and congestion. They climbed the steps stained with dried gum and grime, entered the library, cut across the cool, spacious lobby, and headed down to the basement auditorium where their conversation was to take place. After greeting the American writers who soon arrived one after another, Sejin, Haeri, and Jungeun climbed onto the stage with them. The small auditorium could seat about fifty people, but not even half the seats were filled. While she listened to the moderator give the introduction, Sejin found herself looking for Norman among the mostly Asian audience members. It was much later that she realized Norman would now be in his sixties.

The Korean War, the division of Korea, Inter-Korean Exchanges, North Korean literature . . . North Korean literature? I'm afraid I don't know much about the subject. To be honest, I haven't given it much thought, do you have books from North Korea? I heard the United States has actively undertaken the translation of North Korean literature and has the largest collection in the world. The conversation continued in English and Korean as they moved on to the effects of Korea's democratization, state violence, and non-regularization of labor after the IMF crisis on Korean creatives, and how the 2016 Candlelight Protests, the experiences in Gwanghwamun Square, and the impeachment of the Korean president have informed their respective genres and practices. At the end, when the moderator asked the panelists if they had any questions for one another, they looked at each other in bewilderment. There were a few attempts at trivial questions and responses that were closer to jokes, and after everyone laughed, the moderator turned it over to the audience. A thin woman sitting close to the exit raised her hand. Her straight black hair, which was in a loose ponytail, hung over one shoulder, and her face was flushed. I heard you were coming from Korea, so I came to meet you today, she said.

I've been sitting here, listening for an hour and a half, but no one brought up Korean adoptees or the export of Korean adoptees. For an hour and a half, not once did anyone mention it. I need to know.

Why?

•

Sejin was tired of smiling and tired of seeing other people's smiling faces. She wanted to go back to the hotel. As she stood next to those who continued to exchange niceties, she felt a tap on her right shoulder. A woman with bobbed hair and striking eyes stood before her, smiling at

Sejin without saying a word. I'm sorry, but do I know you? Sejin asked, flustered. The woman pressed her own chest with her right thumb and said, I'm Jamie. Jamie Kylie.

Eonni.

That's how Jamie addressed Sejin.

Sejin had never seen a picture of Jamie. All she had was Norman's voice telling her that Jamie was in a car accident, that Jamie needed surgery, that Jamie was fine, that Jamie was doing well, that Jamie said hi, and so on—bits of news and mentions of her name. As soon as Sejin realized who Jamie was, Jamie hunched her shoulders and gave an awkward, close-lipped smile. Sejin was stunned and asked Jamie what she was doing here and how she'd managed to find her. Jamie said nonchalantly that she'd googled her.

Sejin told the others she was taking off and walked out with Jamie. Exposed to the late afternoon sun, the streets bustled with scowling people. The aroma of stir-fry wafted out of open restaurant doors.

Where are you staying?

Brooklyn. At a hotel.

Is that where we're going?

I don't know. I don't know anything around here. Where do you want to go?

Let's head to Brooklyn. I live around there.

Sejin and Jamie took turns walking ahead or behind, as the sidewalk wasn't wide enough for them to walk side by side, and they headed down to the subway station. After waiting on a platform where condensation from the air conditioning dripped down concrete walls and hot air blew in from the vents, they boarded a Brooklyn-bound train that resembled a rusted chest. At Sejin's hotel, they ordered an arugula sandwich, a poached egg salad, and some coffee. They ate slowly. Jamie grinned without saying anything, the left corner of her mouth turned up slightly. She seemed flustered. Whenever the silence went too long, she clasped her coffee mug, peered into it, and took a sip. Her fingertips were puffy with eczema. Sejin wondered if Jamie had taken the afternoon off work and thought that perhaps the smile on her face wasn't actually a smile but an after-effect of the accident. She recalled what she'd heard from Norman—short updates that had mentioned the details. Sejin cut the poached egg with her plastic fork.

So, Jamie said. When are you going back to Korea?

In three days.

That soon?

Yup.

Why?

My girlfriend's in the hospital.

Oh, Jamie said, nodding. How is she?

She's great, but she's not okay. But she's really great.

Every day I feel like I'm failing, Miyeong had said. I want to be able to say something is bad if it's bad, but I have to try so hard, and the harder I try, I get the feeling that I'm failing miserably.

Sejin swallowed the tasteless poached egg. Jamie was studying architecture at Cooper Union on scholarship. Once I graduate, I'll be able to get a good job in New York, but I live in Jersey City right now. In a small apartment. My roommate and I split the rent. Jersey City? Across from Manhattan, across the Hudson River, Jamie said, raising her thumb to point behind her. Sejin told her about her walk by the river early that morning and how she'd seen two beams of light shooting up into the Manhattan sky. Jamie listened to her, nodding, and explained that what she'd seen was the Tribute in Light. Because tomorrow's 9/11.

Ah, Sejin said with a nod.

Jamie set her empty coffee mug on the table, lost in thought. She asked Sejin if she had walked across the Brooklyn Bridge to Manhattan yet. When Sejin said she hadn't, Jamie asked if she wanted to walk across it now. It'll take about two hours in total. Do you think you can do it? Of course, Sejin said. I can do it.

They left the hotel, heading in the opposite direction Sejin had gone that morning, and used the pedestrian walkway in the middle of the street between the car lanes. As the walkway curved toward the river, Sejin saw a stone pier rising above the water. As they got closer to the pier, the walkway, which had been level with the road, rose gradually, finally leading to the pedestrian promenade on the top level of the bridge. The white divider line that separated the pedestrian lane from the bike lane had almost faded away, erased by foot traffic and bicycle tires, with people paying it no attention, walking on either side.

This is really weird.

What's weird?

It's just, sorry, Jamie said. But it's still weird. This, right now.

Yeah, Sejin said.

Jamie said that Norman used to tell her there was someone in Korea who looked exactly like Anna. Sejin realized Anna was Yun Bukyeong's American name. Granny Anna died when I was young. I didn't know her well. I only heard stories about her. Just a few stories. Dad doesn't talk much, but he brought up that day in Korea when Granny Anna met Sunja—yes, your mom—quite a few times. He would suddenly start talking about it. I heard about that day so many times it feels like we've already met. Today's the first time I'm meeting you, but it doesn't feel like it, so it's weird.

Yes, Sejin said. It's the same for me. I feel the same.

A bicycle sped past Sejin, and when she stepped closer to Jamie by half a step, Jamie also moved over by half a step. Sejin could see cars speeding along the roadway under her feet through the wooden planks of the promenade. The wind carried the briny smell of the river mixed with the exhaust fumes from the roadway, turning the air acrid and damp. There was a stuffy feeling in Sejin's chest, as if she didn't have enough air. She walked slowly. That's the Chrysler building over there. Sejin looked where Jamie pointed and easily found the building. The spire, which seemed so small and delicate next to the other buildings, shimmered in the afterglow of the sun. Jamie said the Chrysler Building was an asset of Cooper Union and that until a few years ago, the school used the income it generated to offer a full-tuition scholarship to every student.

But not anymore?

No, not anymore.

They crossed the bridge to Manhattan and walked toward City Hall. After crossing Broadway and continuing on for about ten minutes, they entered a plaza filled with young oak trees planted at regular intervals. Sejin heard the roar of a waterfall. She walked toward the sound and saw two vast pools.

South Pool and North Pool.

The wide metal parapets around the edge of the pools were inscribed with names. For some time, Sejin watched people in sunglasses stick roses into the grooved names and bow their heads. She then walked toward the parapets. Many of the names had white, red, and yellow roses stuck in them. The water under the parapets cascaded down the wall into a square basin, and then from there dropped once more, flowing into a deep void in the center of the pool. From where Sejin stood, she couldn't see how deep it was or where it went. It seemed it would look the same to everyone, no matter where they stood at the pool or how tall they were.

At first Sejin thought they were more like waterfalls than pools, but in the end, she decided they were indeed pools. The architect of the memorial was determined to make everyone witness this void that could never be filled, even if water flowed eternally into it. Therefore, they were pools.

Pools that thousands upon thousands of tons of water could not fill, that eons of time could never complete or silence.

That no one knew the depth of, that no one could ever know.

A luxury city, Miyeong had said. Sejin recalled this.

That's what the narrator had called it, in a promotional video produced to persuade people who were against the creation of a memorial park in Ansan to commemorate the victims of the Sewol ferry disaster. Miyeong said she'd heard the narrator's voice somewhere, her low, calm voice, which narrated the video that unfolded in soft, vibrant colors at a relaxed pace, reminiscent of calm breathing. The narrator explained the memorial park would be a facility that would benefit the city, that it wouldn't be an ossuary that would bring down real-estate prices, and that with this park, our city would be reborn as a luxury city.

A luxury city.

Miyeong said the narrator had probably cried before and after speaking those words because they'd made her say them.

I can't forgive them.

•

With Norman next time, Sejin said. Come to Korea with Norman next time.

Jamie smiled, nodding slowly, and then shook her head. She said that Norman wouldn't be going to Korea anymore.

Eonni. You know the word *yanggalbo*?

Jamie said Norman grew up in an area with a Korean community.

Anna heard it all the time from the local Koreans. That she must have been a Yankee whore, otherwise, how else could she have met an American soldier who'd been stationed in Korea when she couldn't speak a word of English? I think they had their own complex about Anna. They believed Anna was the one who upset them, but it was probably their own thoughts about the motherland that bothered them. They were probably worried about how they appeared to real Americans because of women like Anna. Maybe they were jealous, assuming she had an unfair advantage on immigrant life. Anna didn't get along with those Koreans. Norman, though, played with their kids and that's how he heard those things. Your mom's a Yankee whore, she's a Yankee bride, they'd say in Korean. Norman came home and asked Anna, Yanggalbo, yangsaekshi—what does it mean? After that, they learned that those kids and their parents talked about Anna at home. He learned that the adults he saw at church on Sundays said those things about Anna, about his mom.

My dad doesn't like Korea. He doesn't like the language or the people.

According to my mother, my dad didn't get along with Anna either. He's always been that way, and he still is. He just doesn't get along with people. He and my mom separated a long time ago. Did I tell you he hardly talks? He's a man of few words. I think the older he gets, the harder and more embarrassing he finds talking.

Two years ago when I went to visit him in the summer, I saw him sweat just trying to ask for a scoop of lemon sherbet at the ice cream parlor. That's why I was so surprised when he called to say you were coming to New York and asked me to meet you. I'm curious. What does he say when you talk to him?

Do you know your dad can speak Korean?

I've known since I was young. A few incidents made me realize he understood Korean. He knows, because it's his mother tongue. Because Anna must have soothed him and rocked him to sleep in Korean. So yes, Eonni, my dad knows how to speak Korean, but he doesn't ever speak it. I can speak Korean. Only a little, but I can. Not because he taught me. I learned it as an adult. After hearing about Anna from my mom. After hearing what Anna told my mom.

I think about it sometimes.

Yanggalbo, yangsaekshi.

My dad couldn't forgive the people who said those things, so he decided he wouldn't forgive the language they used either. He wouldn't forgive the people who had shunned, ignored, and disrespected Anna, and their language. But to me, it seems like a strong sense of identification. With the people who called Anna a Yankee whore. He despised Anna's language, his own mother tongue.

When I was young, my dad used to say there was a person in Korea who looked exactly like Anna. He said that if Anna had lived in Korea, she would have had a different life, a happier, less lonely life, but I don't think so. Anna lived her life, here.

Matt Kylie, my dad's dad, was a womanizer. Did you ever hear what Anna did? She went to his military base and met his superior officer. She jabbed him in the chest and said, You, because you can't manage your men, my home, my family is being destroyed. Because you are not doing your job. In broken English, mixing in Korean profanities. My mom told me this story and laughed, saying Anna knew a thing or two. She knew exactly where to strike to get someone like Grandpa Matt to fall in line.

•

After saying goodbye to Jamie, who had to cross the Hudson River to get to Jersey City, Sejin walked back across the Brooklyn Bridge alone. She stopped by a store to buy some water and found donut peaches, which she also bought, before heading back to the hotel. Someone from her group had left a message saying they were at a nearby bar and invited her to join them if she wished. She'd also received a few photos of the cat from the cat-sitter. Sejin wondered if Jamie made it safely to Jersey City or if she had messaged, but there were no new messages after the initial "hi!" Jamie had sent when they'd exchanged phone numbers. Sejin made a call to Korea and asked to speak to Miyeong. When Miyeong asked about her day, Sejin said she was asked an embarrassing question she'll never live down, that she apologized for her ignorance, that she met Jamie, a distant relative, that they took a walk together, that Jamie was tall, taller than her, and that she called her Eonni, as if it were her name.

Miyeong seemed to be considering everything she'd said.

What are you doing tomorrow?

We're going out tomorrow. Somewhere north of Manhattan Valley. I saw it on a map. There's a place around there called Hell's Kitchen. It's actually called that—Hell's Kitchen.

My god, Miyeong said. Take lots of pictures.

Okay.

Be careful.

All right.

Good night.

Sejin hung up and walked into the bathroom. She turned on the tap and scrubbed the donut peaches under running water and ate one standing at the sink. The donut peach was soft and juicy, and she felt she could go on eating them. She ate until she was full and collected the pits and threw them into the trash bin under the sink, then stepped into the shower. She shampooed her hair, washed her body, and brushed her teeth. She sat by the window until her hair was almost dry, fluffed her pillow by hitting it a few times, and then lay down on the bed. Savoring the taste of peach that lingered in her mouth even after brushing her teeth, she closed her eyes and waited for sleep to come. Someone in the next room turned on the television. Brooklyn, Coney, Staten, Manhattan, Jersey City.

Anna lived her life here.

In *Things to Come*, Fabien and Nathalie meet as student and teacher, and continue their friendship as colleagues, but they argue because of irreconcilable views. Miyeong often said the movie poster was deceiving. In the original poster, the two characters are walking together, looking in completely different directions, lost in their own thoughts, but in the Korean poster, they are smiling softly at each other. Wearing black shorts, a rumpled T-shirt, and slip-on shoes, Fabien has his hand on Nathalie's left shoulder, and is bringing his face close to hers, as if about to kiss her. Nathalie, too, is leaning toward Fabien. They look like lovers who have just reunited at the train station, but the purpose of this reunion is Nathalie's rattan basket, and the two are not romantically involved. For those who first encounter the film through this poster, they might expect a romance to blossom between these two characters, but it never happens. They don't fall in love. Miyeong said this is what she loved the most about the movie.

The only person who experiences romance in *Things to Come* is Heinz, who is Nathalie's husband. At the beginning of the movie, he announces he has fallen in love, and packs his things and leaves, ending his marriage with Nathalie. When she finds out that he has taken the books that they'd shared, Nathalie is enraged. But Nathalie is busy. Terribly busy. She is still busy at the end of the film when Heinz appears in her kitchen while she is cooking an extravagant dinner. She is so busy she even appears to have forgiven Heinz, but when he complains of loneliness and asks if he can stay for dinner, she is horrified and brushes him off.

In *Things to Come*, Mia Hansen-Løve does a perfect job of dashing any hope of romance and reconciliation, disappointing those who had been hoping for those things. Miyeong said she really liked this aspect of the film.

Miyeong was right, Sejin thought.

Even if she doesn't do those things, life goes on, busily.

Busy Nathalie.

While she weeps, while she is disappointed, while she loses hope, while she rages. In other words, while she loves.

Because those things are coming to Nathalie.

Because they are always coming, Miyeong said.

afterword

Through the years, I've met many women with the name Sunja.

Why are there so many Sunjas?

This book began with that question.

"Nameless" was written after hearing the story of Sunja, who was born in 1946, and how she fled south during the Korean War.

During the interview process, she and I both realized her narrative was disjointed. The object of her sentence often disappeared, the time and place became jumbled, and her sentences rarely went on for more than five words. Each time, she would gasp out a few words, suddenly stop, and then stare at me.

While writing "Nameless," there was a point when I thought I should write it the way Sunja spoke. However, I put an end to my efforts. Still, I decided to keep some of my efforts in the story.

I will not forget the things that happened to me while I wrote *Years and Years*.

With each story I wrote, I lived a life, in the way you only could through a story, and I found it both wonderful yet terrifying.

Would people read this as a family story?

There was a time I was curious about these things, and to be honest, I'm still curious.

No matter how this book might be read, I hope it will be what you need.

I'm grateful to Sunja, who shared her story with me,

to Kim Sunyoung, who gave me sage advice and encouragement until the very end,

to those I think about often,

and to those who will read this book someday.

I wish you all

a long and happy life.

Hwang Jungeun
2020